Praise for *Cutthroat*

"Paul Heatley remains a master of savagery, of bloody men and how they live, how they die, how they kill."

—Rob Pierce, author of *Tommy Shakes*

Praise for Paul Heatley

"Heatley is becoming a master of American noir in the vein of Jim Thompson and James M. Cain."

—David Nemeth

CUTTHROAT

Books by Paul Heatley

PAUL HEATLEY

CUTTHROAT

All Due Respect
An imprint of Down & Out Books
3959 Van Dyke Road, Suite 265
Lutz, FL 33558
DownAndOutBooks.com

Cover design by Zach McCain

ISBN: 1-64396-107-1
ISBN-13: 978-1-64396-107-1

For Aidan

Part One
Newcastle
1978

Chapter One

There were no pictures on John Riddell's walls. No framed photographs of family members on the window sills or the electric fire's mantelpiece. He didn't own records. He didn't have a television. There were no books. The paint on the walls was peeling. There was a patch of damp in the top-left corner of the ceiling opposite the front door.

The only thing close to approaching decoration could be the naked woman lying on the bed, writhing on the crumpled bed sheets, waiting for him to undress.

There were only three rooms. A sitting room/kitchen. Bedroom. Bathroom. The bathroom stank of mould. John didn't take care of his home. It looked like he was ready to up and leave at a moment's notice. Likely, he was. Leave the city the same way he arrived.

No one knew much about him, other than his appearance and temperament. He was a big man, broad-shouldered and big-knuckled. He was laid back. He took the piss out of people he knew, and those he didn't. He was calm. Until he wasn't. And when he wasn't, no one wanted to be around him. He left chaos the equivalent of a bomb blast. And though people couldn't be sure when he'd first arrived in Newcastle and started making a name for himself, they knew he was a Geordie, if only through his accent. No one could claim to have gone to school with him. No one had knocked around with him in their youth. No one knew who his parents or extended family were. There were stories that he'd been in borstal, the explanation as to why he was such a mystery man, but John would neither confirm nor deny anything.

Even the woman on his bed knew little about him beyond his name, appearance, and her attraction for him.

She wasn't his girlfriend.

Wasn't his wife, either.

Her name was Mary Irons.

She was someone's wife. The only item she still wore was her wedding ring.

"You gonna take much longer, then?" she said, propping herself up on her elbows.

John undid the buttons on his shirt, hung it from a hanger on the back of his bedroom door. "Just admiring the view, pet."

Mary looked him over in turn. His body was mostly muscle, though a little softer in the midsection. A few scars that looked like slashes from a knife on his left shoulder, and another across his right pectoral. She'd asked about them, the first time. His answer had been simple. "Fighting."

"I don't have all night," Mary said.

"We've got long enough," John said. He winked at her, loosened his belt buckle.

"I like it slow."

"I know exactly how you like it."

She giggled, spread her legs a little wider as he stepped out of his pants. He hooked them through the hanger with the shirt, then climbed onto the bed with her, into her arms and between her legs.

After, they lay together and shared a cigarette. "I've gotta get away in a minute," John said.

"See? Telt ye there was a rush." Mary drew on the cigarette, held it up to his lips.

"And I told you we had time. And we did."

"Who you gotta go see?"

"Your fella. That's how I knew there wasn't any rush."

Mary sat up a little. "Shit, where at?"

"Nowhere near here, divvint worry. I'll be goin into town."

She settled down, the back of her head resting on his scarred shoulder. "Got some business goin?"

"Could be. Divvint kna yet, but only time he ever wants to see me is when there's a job in the works. He mentioned anything to you?"

"He never talks about that stuff with me."

"What about yer dad? He ever mention anything?"

"Nah, nowt."

"What about when you were a little girl? Did he regale you with stories of his daring daylight robbery exploits?"

"Never saw him when I was a bairn. He was usually locked up."

"I'm sure you went to visit."

"Depended where they had him. Sometimes it was just me mam went down, left us with me grandma for a few days. Whenever I did see him he was never talking about what he'd done. It was all, *Divvint worry pet, I'll be out before you know it.*" She deepened her voice in an approximation of her father's. John had to admit it was a good impression. "*And I'll never get caught again, promise.* Aye, that's what he said. Never promised to go on the straight and narrow so there'd be no excuse to lock him up. Promised never to get *caught* again."

John chuckled, finished the cigarette and stubbed it out against the wall next to the headboard, dumped the butt on the sill to clear away later.

"I'm getting chilly," Mary said, rubbing her arms. "It's always bloody freezing in this flat. I dunno how you stand it."

"Hard as nails, man."

"I don't doubt it."

"That and I'm always out. Busy boy. Only ever here with you, really."

Mary swung her legs over the side of the bed, gathered up her underwear and dress. "I'm flattered. Our little love nest. Special little place all our own."

"Glad you approve. Love nest—that's exactly what I was aiming for." John went to the door, put back on the clothes he'd recently taken off.

"You ever thought about decorating? Fresh lick of paint?"

John shrugged. "What's the point?"

"Make it feel like a home, that's the point."

"This whole block's rough as a badger's arse, man. Nowt homely about it."

"Not with that attitude."

"Not with any attitude."

"Whey, y'kna, it's not like we're on the Riviera. But we *are* on the Tyne. No reason why we can't improve our own personal surroundings and make it something special."

"I've never been to the Riviera, but I reckon it's canny different to the Tyne."

"I've never been either, but aye, you're probably right. And you know the point I'm trying to make."

"*Trying* to make."

Mary took a seat on the edge of the bed, pulled on her heels. "So. That's something new I know about you now."

John raised an eyebrow. "What's that?"

"You've never been to France."

"I've never been to the Riviera. Never said I hadn't been to France."

"*Have* you?"

John said nothing.

"Oh, howay, man! It's just a place. You can tell

us that much."

John shrugged. "I've been all over, me. Can't keep track of them all."

Mary shook her head, grinned, got to her feet and went to him. She put her hands on his chest, kissed him. "You'd better get a move on," she said. "And I'd better get away back home."

John grunted. "I'll see you soon."

"If you're lucky."

Mary left the building first. John stood by the window, watched her pass by on the street below. Waited five minutes. He didn't have to rush. Didn't mind making them wait.

He headed to the pub on foot, lit a cigarette on the way. Daniel Irons and Malcolm Reay sat in a corner, talking over pints. John took a seat with them, cigarette dangling from the corner of his mouth. "Didn't get me a drink, like, lads?"

Daniel looked at him, unimpressed. "Didn't know when you were gonna feel like fuckin showing up, did we?"

Malcolm cleared his throat. "You all right, John-lad? Where've you been?"

"Shagging."

Malcolm laughed. Daniel didn't look impressed.

He'd look less impressed if he'd known John had been shagging his wife.

Of course, he never looked impressed anyway. Had the perpetually severe face of a miserable bastard that never cracked a smile. John reckoned he was a real barrel of laughs at home. No wonder Mary came to see him.

Malcolm was more laid back. A modern kind of guy with long hair, a moustache, flared pants. He took a sip of his beer. Froth stuck to the hair on his top lip. He licked it off.

"We gonna be here long, or what?" John said.

"Long enough for you to get yerself a pint, if that's what you're asking," Daniel said.

"Canny. Then I'll be right back. Divvint gan anywhere."

Daniel glared at him, but said nothing.

John went to the bar, waited to be served. The atmosphere was thick and smoky, an asthmatic's nightmare. John lit another cigarette, ordered his pint. He glanced back at Daniel and Malcolm in the corner. They were talking again. Daniel was probably complaining about him, his attitude, being late. Let him complain. They needed John more than John needed them.

"Crack then, lads?" John said, sitting back down.

Daniel stared at him. "You ready? You sure?"

"Good to go."

Daniel took a long breath through his nose. "What're you messin around, for? You think I'd call you here if this wasn't work related? I'm not lookin to fuckin socialise with ye."

"I know that, Daniel. I wouldn't wanna hear from you if it wasn't work related."

Daniel bristled. "You think this isn't serious? You

got somethin better to be doin?"

"I've *always* got somethin better to be doin, mate. I'm an in-demand lad. It's a privilege for you to have me here sittin with you."

Daniel ran his tongue round the inside of his mouth like there was a bad taste there. "I divvint like you, John."

John shrugged.

"I divvint like yer attitude. Yer a cocky bastard, that's all you are. We don't need you."

"You waited an awful long time for me to get here if you don't need me." John grinned.

Malcolm concentrated on his pint, stayed out of their heated discussion.

"You're a two-bit heavy, that's all," Daniel said. "You're nowt special. We can find another like you just like that." He clicked his fingers.

"Aye, well, I'm here now so why don't we just get on with it, eh? Course, if you're that bothered, maybe you could have a chat with yer father-in-law, see what he has to say. The Top Man."

The Top Man. Steven Edwards. Mary's father.

Daniel gritted his teeth at that. John had done plenty of jobs for Steven down the years, and he'd had no complaints.

John cocked his head. "No?"

Malcolm put his hands down flat on the table, playing peacekeeper. "Why don't we just get on with it, eh? We're all here now, let's just get this thing sorted."

Daniel and John stared at each other, then Daniel broke his gaze and shifted in his seat. "Aye, all right."

John sat back, smiled.

Daniel popped his knuckles. John wondered if he was supposed to be intimidated. "It happens in three days," he said. "Are you paying attention?"

John winked.

Daniel went over the plan. When he'd finished, he looked at them both. "Got that?" Malcolm nodded enthusiastically. John raised his eyebrows.

"Good," Daniel said. "And I shouldn't have to say this, but divvint be fuckin late the day of, eh? You reckon you can do that?"

"I'm a professional, Dan."

"Aye, so you claim."

"You've seen me in action."

"Aye, and yet I still feel like I've gotta keep on at you about doing things the right fuckin way. Funny that, isn't it?"

"You're too uptight."

"The fuckin two of ye are too uptight," Malcolm said, eyes wide. "Jesus Christ, feels like I'm sitting in the middle of a pissing contest here. Lookit, we'll get the job done, it'll gan off without a hitch, it'll be fine. Everything'll be fine, all right?"

"You don't need to persuade me," John said. "I already know."

Daniel ground his teeth. Whenever John was round him—and this predated his involvement with Mary—he always seemed to be itching for a fight.

John wasn't sure if that was a trait particular to when he was nearby, or if that was how Daniel went on with everyone. Either way, John would be more than happy to oblige him, if he ever wanted to get down and dirty and throw some fists. Plenty had stepped up before, none of them had walked away intact.

"Well." Daniel finished his pint. "We'll just have to find out together, won't we? But I'll tell you this now, John—three days' time, if you're late, I'm out. You understand? I'll be walking away. I'm not putting myself at risk over your bullshit. I won't put myself at risk for *anyone*."

"Fair enough," John said. "Neither would I."

"Whatever. I'm goin home." He got to his feet.

"Reckon I'll stay out for a few more," John said. He looked round the room. "Might go somewhere with a bit more life to it than this shithole, though."

Malcolm grinned. John turned to him.

"What about you, Malc? You gotta get home and away to bed like some auld gadgy, or are you up for hitting the Toon?"

"Whey, I'm definitely up for a few more drinks, like," Malcolm said. "It's a Tuesday though, I divvint reckon anywhere else is gonna be much livelier than this."

"We'll just have to take our chances, then. See what the night brings us."

Daniel looked between the two of them as they spoke. He was standing, but he hadn't left the table yet. "Listen, if either of you turn up hungover an'all, it's off. And I'll be very pissed. And you can bet yer arse the Top Man will be pissed, too."

"You think it'll take us three days to shake a hangover?" John said.

"It worries me that maybe you'll not stop drinking for three fuckin days."

John and Malcolm exchanged glances. "We'll show him," Malcolm said. "Let's gan for four!"

"Divvint let his bad influence rub off on you, Malcolm."

Malcolm laughed. "Trust me, mate, I've had me fill of bad influences. There's not a bad decision I've never not made."

"I know." Daniel nodded, solemn. "I've seen some of your lasses."

John laughed. He had to hand it to Daniel. That one was funny.

Daniel left. John resisted the urge to tell him to say hello to Mary for him. It wasn't worth the trouble.

"So," Malcolm said. "Where we gonna go?"

John downed his pint, started getting to his feet. "Anywhere that isn't fuckin here."

Chapter Two

Malcolm propped himself up on the bar. They'd hit three pubs and he was already worse for wear. John felt fine. He sipped his fresh pint. "You can't handle your drink that well, can you?"

Malcolm waved him off, lowered himself until the side of his face rested on the counter. "I'm fine, man. I'm fine." His eyes closed. Strands of his long hair began to soak up the spilled beer there.

"It surprises me, Malcolm. I thought you were out and about all the time. Every other night, I thought."

Malcolm grunted. "I pace meself."

"I'm hardly storming through."

Malcolm grunted again, harder this time. "Piss off, man."

"You look like you're about to fall asleep."

"Just resting me eyes."

"You want me to call you a taxi?"

"Nah, man. I said I'm fine. Just give us five minutes' peace, will ye?"

John grinned to himself. "You want to find a seat,

or are you happy where you are?"

Malcolm straightened up, breathing deep through his nose as he did so. The wet hair spread itself across his face, stuck there. He winced at it, curled his lip, wiped it away. "I can stand just fine," he said. He got the attention of the bartender, ordered another round of pints for himself and John. He turned back to John, his eyes half-closed. "Night's still young, man. Y'kna, Daniel never wants to gan out on the piss like this. Not properly, not anymore. Like he gans out a lot, but on his own. Between you and me, I think he goes on the pull…"

From what John knew of Daniel and Mary's relationship, this didn't surprise him. "You and him old friends, eh?"

"Oh, aye. Went to school together and that. Done everything together. I was best man at his wedding."

"He stopped wanting to go out with the lads since he tied the knot, that it?"

"Nah, nah, Mary's not got anything to do with it. She's canny. She'd be out every other night, if he'd let her. I dunno, the two of them, ever since the whole miscarriage thing…Whatever, man, it's not my place to say. It's just the way he is, that's all. He's a right miserable cunt sometimes. Forgets he's allowed to have fun."

"Why's that, then?"

Malcolm shrugged, took his new pint from the bartender, nearly spilled it raising it to his mouth. He widened his eyes, steadied himself. "I dunno, like.

He's always been intense. That's what he was like at school, an'all. Had this proper angry face all the time. Probably cos of his dad."

"What about his dad?"

"His dad's dead now. Doesn't matter."

"He was angry because his dad had died?"

"Nah, man. When he was younger, he was angry because his dad was still alive. *He* was an angry bastard, an'all. A proper cunt. I reckon he used to knock Daniel round a bit."

"Oh, aye?"

"Daniel never said as much, but I saw some bruises on him sometimes. Saw them on his mam, an'all. And he was a right nasty auld bastard. Chased me a couple of times."

"What for?"

"Divvint kna, didn't stop to ask. Think he was drunk, but who could fuckin tell. He was always bloody drunk. Always lookin for a fight, too. That's probably why he gave me a chase. Wanted to give us a hiding. That kind of bloke. I hated going round to Daniel's house, not that I had to that often. Daniel hated being there, so he usually came to mine. Stayed late. Like he didn't wanna leave."

"How'd the bloke die?"

"Few winters ago now, slipped on some ice when he was heading home from the pub. Cracked the back of his head open, lay there and died. All alone."

"Daniel and his mam, devastated by it, were they?"

"Nah, not at all. Put their sad faces on for the

funeral, but they didn't give a shit, not really. They were glad."

John took a look round the rest of the room. He always made a point to stay aware of his surroundings. Took notice if people moved and where they went. A couple of blokes in the corner had caught his eye a few times already. Seemed like every time he glanced in their direction, they were quick to look away, as if they'd been watching him and Malcolm. He wondered if they were police. Doubted it, though. Too short, too fat. Shirt sleeves rolled up to reveal blurry tattoos, so faded John couldn't be sure what the original designs were supposed to be. More than likely they'd had a few pints and were looking for trouble. John marked them in his peripheral, stayed aware of their movements.

"He's all right though, really," Malcolm said. "Daniel is. I don't want it to sound like I'm calling him, cos I'm not. He's a good lad. Here, how long've we been out now?"

John shrugged. "Couple of hours."

"Wor lass is gonna kill us." Malcolm laughed. "Not be the first time she's been ready to try. Has a gan at us every other week, feels like."

"She expecting you earlier?"

"Whey, I telt her I'd be an hour. I think that was about four ago, now. It's not that she'll be mad I'm late, just that she didn't get an invite."

"Wife?"

"Nah, girlfriend. We've only been together, uh…" Malcolm looked to the ceiling, did his maths.

"Six months now."

"And you're living together already?"

"Not officially. She stays over. She stays over more often than not."

"What's her name?"

"Tina. Tina Watson. Sometimes I call her Tina Turner, cos you should see her legs." Malcolm wiggled his eyebrows. "She's not black, though. She's a pale Geordie lass. And a blonde. Looks like a rock star. She loves Bowie and that. Roxy Music. We saw Bowie, actually. Back in June."

"She looking for a future in music, is she?"

"Nah, modelling."

John had never seen Malcolm's girlfriend before—had never heard of her before this conversation—but now he was curious. "She a looker, is she?"

"Not really." Malcolm laughed. "But she's got big dreams. I admire that. And she's got those legs. She could maybe get work as a shoe model. Or like, I dunno, dresses. Anything from the neck down. I mean, she's not ugly, mind. But her teeth are a mess." Malcolm shrugged. "I dunno. What am I even talkin about?"

"Your lass."

"Aye, I kna that. I mean..." He giggled, took another drink, confusing himself. "I love wor lass. She's the best. My little Tina Turner."

"Did she make you dress up for Bowie?"

"Nah, but you should've seen her. The works. All that colourful shit round her eyes and that. Went

18

along looking like Ziggy Stardust. He wasn't that colourful, mind. Still doin the whole Thin White Duke thing. D'you keep up with his music?"

"I hear him, here and there. I don't keep up with him. Don't keep up with anyone. Don't know that many Tina Turner songs, either."

"Bloody hell, John. What d'you do for fun, then?"

John held up his pint. "Yer lookin at it. And what we're doin in three days' time."

"Aye, that *is* fun. And better'n an actual fuckin job."

"Keep your voice down."

"Oh, sorry. Am I loud? I get drunk, I can't control me volume."

"No, you're fine, no one heard. Just keep it that way."

John saw movement out the corner of his eye. The two men that had been watching them the whole time they'd been in the pub. They'd got to their feet, were coming over. Malcolm hadn't seen them. The bigger of the two led the way. The other followed obediently behind. They both had their mean faces on. John turned himself to face them.

"Right, lads," said the big man. "We've waited long enough. Yer long-haired mate, we want him out, now."

The bartender watched their approach, heard their words, but said nothing. Stepped back and folded his arms, allowed whatever was about to happen to unfold.

Malcolm was aware of their presence now. He turned. "You talkin about me?"

"I divvint see any other fuckin long-haired poufters in here."

Malcolm smirked. "None with long hair, nah."

The big man's eyes narrowed. "You've got some fuckin nerve, for a pillow biter." He turned back to John. "Get yer rent boy out, *now*, before we smash yer fuckin faces in. Get out, and divvint ever come back. We divvint want the likes of you lot in here. It isn't that kind of bar."

John took a drink. Took his time about it.

The big man rolled his shoulders. "Are you takin the piss, mate? You think we're having a laugh, here?"

John put down his glass.

Malcolm straightened up suddenly. "Here—are you callin *me* a pouf?"

"You catch on fast, you little mincer."

Malcolm took a swing at the big man, but his coordination was off and his throw was sloppy. The punch caught the big man with a glancing blow on the cheek. The big man blinked at him.

"Calm down, Malcolm," John said. "And you two fuck off back to your seats. We'll leave when we're good and ready."

"I wasn't asking, mate."

"I'm not your fuckin mate. Now fuck off. *I* wasn't asking."

The big man took a step closer, opened his mouth, jabbed a fat finger into John's face. He didn't get a chance to speak again. John grabbed the finger, twisted it back. There was the sound of a dry twig snapping. The big man screamed. His friend's eyes went wide. He took a step back. The big man fell to his knees. John still had hold of the finger. Twisted it a little more. Then he started punching. The blows stifled the big man's screams. They closed his eyes, bloodied his mouth, broke his nose.

Something caught the light out the corner of John's eye, flashed. He looked up. The big man's friend had pulled a knife. John grinned. He spread his hand wide on the big man's bloodied face, pushed him to the ground, and straightened up.

The friend cut the air with the knife. "Howay, then! Howay then, ya fuckin cunt!"

"He's got a knife, John!" Malcolm said.

John ignored him.

"Howay, lads, that's enough," the bartender said, though he didn't step any closer to them, just raised his hands in a peacemaking gesture.

Others in the pub were looking over, but none of them made any effort to come closer, either. No one wanted to get cut.

"You keep swinging that knife at me," John said, "I'm gonna take it off ye and cut ya fingers off. That clear?"

The friend didn't lower the knife. John looked down at the big man. He'd rolled onto his side, was clutching at his broken finger and groaning, spitting teeth and blood.

"He said put the fuckin thing down, ya deaf cunt!" Malcolm pushed himself off the bar, shoved the friend, grabbed for the knife. They scuffled. The friend fended him off with his free arm. He struck with his right, with the knife. It caught Malcolm along the forearm. Tore through his jacket and shirt sleeve. There was a spray of blood. "Jesus Christ!" Malcolm fell back, clutched at his arm. Blood ran through his fingers.

John stepped forward, took the knife from the friend while he was distracted by what he'd done. He head-butted the friend, put him down. Got on top of him, pinned his left wrist with his knee. "I warned you," he said, then cut off the index finger of his left hand.

The friend screamed. A groan went through the bar. The bartender started shouting something, but John couldn't hear what he was saying. He cut off the middle finger. The friend was pawing at him, trying to get him to stop. He was crying, begging. Blood squirted from the stumps. "I'm gonna shove these up your fuckin arse, pal," John said, spitting words through gritted teeth. He pressed the blade to the ring finger. There was a wedding ring there. John drew a line of blood underneath it, closest to the palm.

"John, mate," Malcolm said.

John stopped cutting, looked up. Malcolm was pale, looked woozy.

"I think we've gotta go, mate," Malcolm said.

Chapter Three

John got a taxi to take them to Gosforth. Malcolm told him the address, then closed his eyes on the backseat.

"Here, make sure yer marra doesn't get blood all over me seat, mind," the driver said.

"Faster you get us there, less time he has to bleed," John said.

The taxi dropped them off outside the house. It was in darkness. John paid the driver then helped Malcolm out, draped his arm over his shoulders and dragged him to the front door. "Will he be in?"

Malcolm cleared his throat. "It's late, he should be. He's always in. We usually call ahead first, though."

"Let's hope he's a light sleeper, then." John started knocking, pounding his fist against the door. Malcolm rapped his knuckles against it too, trying to help, to wake the sleeper inside. His efforts were weak, barely brushed against the wood.

John kept it up, pounding until lights finally came on inside. He eased off. The door opened a crack, the chain still on. A face peered out. "Who the fuck are you?"

John shifted his weight, positioned Malcolm so he was in view.

"I got cut, Doc," Malcolm said.

"Malcolm?" The face looked him over. The door closed. The chain rattled. The door opened wide. "Get him in," the doctor said. "Through to the kitchen, that way. Yous are supposed to call ahead, y'kna. You've probably woken up half the bloody street."

John made it through to the kitchen, pulled out a chair at the dining table and lowered Malcolm into it. He turned to the doctor, took him in fully.

He was in his pyjamas, a long dressing gown over the top of them. He looked a little older than John, late thirties perhaps. They'd never met, but John had heard about him. Dr Doug Mitchell, put the lads back together if they ever got hurt and couldn't go to the hospital for fear of the coppers being called. Broken bones, the occasional gunshot wound, cuts and stabbings. He'd set them, stitch them up, give them the necessary drugs he was able to acquire through his own contacts.

"What's happened to him?" Doug said.

"Slashed with a knife," John said. "Down the right arm there."

Malcolm struggled out of his jacket, rolled up his sleeve. Congealed blood peeled away with it, fresh blood began to pour from the wound. Doug checked it. "Shite," he said. "All right, I'll gan get me gear."

He grabbed a kitchen towel, threw it at John. "Press that on it for now. Try to keep the mess off the floor, an'all."

John went to Malcolm and wrapped the towel around his bleeding forearm, pressed on it hard. The towel soaked through fast. Doug went upstairs. John heard his steps. Shortly after that, he heard conversation, too. Muffled voices. Then raised voices. A woman. John guessed it to be the doctor's wife. Not pleased with their presence at such a late hour.

Malcolm chuckled. "You hear that?"

"Aye. Hard not to. She doesn't sound happy."

"That's why we're supposed to ring ahead."

"Didn't know the number. Didn't have the time."

John couldn't make out much of what was being said above them. Was only able to pick out the anger in the tone. He caught the last part though, from the woman. "Then patch them up and bloody well kick them out!"

A door slammed.

Malcolm looked up at John, raised his eyebrows and pulled a face like a naughty schoolboy hearing something he wasn't supposed to. A couple of moments passed before they heard Doug come back down the stairs. He entered the kitchen carrying a black leather satchel. He hadn't bothered to change out of his dressing gown and pyjamas. He put the bag down on the table. "Yous hear that, did ye?"

"Some of it," John said.

"That's why you're supposed to call first."

"So I've been told."

Doug reached into his bag, started pulling things out. "Whey, yous didn't wake the bairns up, at least."

He threaded a needle, then removed the towel from Malcolm's arm. "I washed me hands already," he said. "You divvint need to worry about that." He shoved the filthy towel in Malcolm's mouth, then poured alcohol over the wound. Malcolm bit down on the towel, screamed into it. "Yer a big boy, ye can take it." Doug wiped the wound clean enough for him to get to work, then stuck the needle through the puckered flesh, started sewing it closed.

John went into the kitchen, got himself a glass of water, drank it down. He refilled it, carried it through for Malcolm.

Doug got halfway through the wound before he spoke again. "So, who're you then? Don't think we've met before."

"No," John said. "We haven't."

"You new?"

"No. Just haven't needed to visit you before."

"Look after yerself, eh? Tough guy."

"Aye."

"Divvint give nowt away, do ye?"

"Not if I can help it."

Doug grinned. "I'm nearly done here."

"I divvint think I'm gonna be able to drive, John," Malcolm said. "Not like this."

"Divvint worry about that now," John said. "We'll deal with that later."

"Daniel's gonna be pissed."

"We'll deal with him later, an'all."

"The two of you stink like a brewery," Doug said. "And Malcolm's obviously drunk. This been a bar fight?"

"Aye," John said.

"It's a clean cut. A knife, you said?"

"Aye."

"Aye, nice and clean. Not a mark on you though, big lad."

"I can handle meself."

"I don't doubt it. You're not the one did the cutting, are ye?"

"Nah, it wasn't John," Malcolm said. "These two other knackers. Should've seen what John here did to them, mind."

John put a hand on Malcolm's shoulder. "The doctor doesn't need to know any more than he needs to. Isn't that right, Doug?"

"Sounds like it," Doug said. He finished up the stitching, wrapped the wound in a bandage. "Keep it dry," he said. "Come back and see me in a couple of weeks, I'll change the dressing, see how it looks. Ring first, mind." He winked.

"How bad is it?" Malcolm said. "Am I gonna lose the use of me fingers or anything?"

"Well, can you use them right now?"

"They tingle a bit, but aye." Malcolm curled and straightened them.

"They'll be fine. Looked worse than it was, wasn't

even that deep. Didn't catch anything serious, skin deep, nowt more."

"Cheers, doc. How pissed off is yer missus?"

Doug shrugged. "She'll get over it. Might take until the Top Man pays us, but she'll get over it."

"We'll get a move on then, Malcolm," John said.

"Aye, straight to home, I hope," Doug said.

"Of course," John said. "Pubs are closed by now."

Chapter Four

Daniel had gone to see her father, so Mary had come to see him.

John had her pressed up against the wall, her legs wrapped around him. They weren't in the bedroom yet. It was the day after Malcolm got cut at the pub. Mary and John didn't often get to see each other two days in a row.

John carried her into the bedroom, still inside. Mary bit his shoulder. He put her onto the bed, pulled out, turned her round. Her underwear was off, but her dress was still on. He drew her knees up, had her on all fours. He slipped back inside. Mary grabbed the headboard. They made it bang.

"Jesus," Mary said when they were done. She fanned herself with her hand, caught her breath. "I saw you last night, man. That was like you'd just got outta prison or somethin."

John stroked her bare thigh. "Guess I missed ye."

She laughed. "How was your night?"

"I'm sure you've heard all about it."

"I've heard about Malcolm's night, and I've heard that you were there. Doesn't look like yours was so bad."

"Unlike Malcolm, I can handle me drink."

"He's always been a bit of a lightweight, despite his best efforts. I heard you handled them two lads an'all."

"How much did you hear?"

"That you beat them up. Malcolm was impressed. Said they were big fellas."

"I've dealt with bigger."

"You're a big lad yerself."

"Not the first time you've told me that."

"I can't be here for long," Mary said. "I don't know how long Daniel will be with me dad for."

"Grassing me up."

"Aye, probably."

"Doesn't matter now, though. Too late in the day for any trouble he might wanna get me into."

"So that meeting last night, there's a job coming up, aye?"

"Aye. Few days from now."

"Me dad knows a lot of lads. He might replace you."

"None of them are as good as me."

"He's fond of Malcolm."

"Malcolm's just a driver. That's all. Replace a driver a lot easier than you can replace the likes of me."

Mary stroked his chest. "So modest." She sat up. "I'm gonna get cleaned up then get away. When do you think you'll hear back from me dad or Daniel?"

"I dunno. Probably soon. Tomorrow maybe. They can't leave it any longer than that."

Mary went through to the bathroom. John stayed on the bed, lit a cigarette. He heard the tap start running. Mary moved round in the bathroom, dried herself with a towel. He heard her go through to the sitting room to find her underwear. "You gonna see me off?"

John got up, walked her to the door. She took the cigarette from his mouth, took a draw from it, put it back between his lips. "I'm sure everything'll be fine. It's just a little cut, isn't it?"

"It'll leave a scar," John said.

"Scars are sexy."

"I'll be sure to let Malcolm know."

Mary kissed him on the side of the mouth. "I'll see you next time." She slipped out the door.

John had asked her once: *What do you tell Daniel if he gets home before you?*

That I was with friends.

He believes that?

Of course. I have friends, *y'kna.*

John took a seat, leaned back in it, the cigarette pointing upward at the ceiling. He remembered the first time he'd met Mary. The first time he met her properly. He'd seen her round a few times before then, but never to talk to. He was dimly aware of her being Daniel's wife, Steven's daughter. It wasn't until Steve's birthday party that he got to talk to her. Their affair started soon after. That was four months ago.

"Well, shit," John said aloud. Four months. Where'd the time go.

Chapter Five

John was pulled before Steven, called to the house. His wife, Denise, answered the door to him. Mary's mother. John could see some resemblance in the face, but that was all. Denise was much fatter. "Are you the one they're all waiting for, pet?"

"Unless they're planning on trying to bollock anyone else today."

"C'mon in, then." She stepped aside, ushered him through to the sitting room. Steven, Daniel and Malcolm were all there. Someone else, too. John didn't recognise him. He stood in the corner, wasn't talking with the others, glanced up briefly at John as he entered then looked away, down at his shoes. He was a big guy. Eyes narrowed. Looked like he was clenching his jaw. If he was Malcolm's replacement, he didn't look like a driver. He was muscle.

"All right, John?" Malcolm said. He smiled.

Steven wasn't smiling, but he wasn't scowling, either.

Daniel was scowling. John wasn't surprised. Had

a face like there was a bad taste in his mouth. Always did.

"All right, John," Steven said, "come and take a seat."

Steven and Daniel occupied chairs on either side of the fireplace. The stranger stood. John lowered himself onto the sofa next to Malcolm.

"Anyone want a cup of tea?" Denise said from the doorway.

"We're all right for now, love," Steven said. "Maybe later. I'll give you a shout."

"All right, pet." Denise went off. John could hear her busying herself in the kitchen.

Mary had Steven's eyes, but luckily nothing else. Got most of her looks from her mother, clearly. Behind Steven, on the mantelpiece, John could see a framed photograph from their wedding day. Denise looked identical to her daughter. Steven looked thinner.

"Got into a bit of bother the other night, did ye?" Steven said.

"Nothing I couldn't handle."

"Oh, I heard all about that."

"I fuckin told you to mind yerself," Daniel said. "I fuckin told ye. The both of you. Keep yer noses clean this close to a fuckin job. You havin a laugh or somethin?"

"We didn't start it," Malcolm said.

"Bet this wanker didn't do anythin to calm it down, neither."

John shrugged.

"Calm down, lads, howay," Steven said. "It's done now."

"It's beside the point," Daniel said.

"And what is the point?"

"The point is this is all a fuckin joke to this prick. He doesn't take anything seriously. He doesn't fuckin *listen*." Daniel was being particularly prickish. His glare had more intensity than usual. John put it down to Malcolm's cut.

"You wanna calm down, son," John said. "You're gonna give yourself high blood pressure goin on like this all the time."

Daniel's eyes widened. A vein bulged in his neck that looked like it was about to burst.

Steven reached over, patted him on the arm. "Calm down man, Daniel. We're not here to fight."

Daniel jabbed a finger at John. "You push my buttons, you do. And you do it on purpose. I'm onto you. Divvint be surprised if you push us too fuckin far one day."

"I'll be sure to keep that in mind, big man."

Daniel looked at his father-in-law, as if willing him to pay witness to the disrespect he was being shown.

Steven waved the two of them quiet. "All right, all right, that's enough. You got anything to say for yerself about what went on, John?"

"Nah, not really. Reckon Malcolm's already told yous everything that happened by now."

"What he could remember."

John grinned. "Sounds about right."

"Hey, that cut sobered me up pretty quick," Malcolm said.

"If anything, it nearly knocked you out."

"Nearly bled us fuckin dry."

"Made you all woozy and that."

"I'm glad the two of you think it's funny," Daniel said. "None of us fuckin do."

"I dunno," Steven said. "It's canny funny."

Daniel stared at his father-in-law, his cheeks reddened, annoyed at Steven showing him up. He took a deep breath, recovered himself, turned back to John and Malcolm. "He can't do the job. Nae good for driving with his arm all wrapped up like that."

Malcolm looked at John, raised his eyebrows, indicated his bandage, shrugged.

"Luckily, Malcolm here had a pal in town," Steven said. He tilted his chin at the man in the corner John didn't recognise. John didn't turn. "This is Jock McCaffery. Happened to be down from bonny Scotland, right in time for us to need him. Handy, eh? Malcolm gave him a call. He's gonna take his place."

"He doesn't look like a driver," John said. Jock was a big guy. Strong. Exuded menace.

"He's not," Daniel said.

"He looks like muscle."

"He is," Daniel said. "Which you'd know if you let us finish. *I'm* gonna be the fuckin driver."

John couldn't help but smile.

"Ye can wipe that fuckin smirk off yer face, an'all."

Steven interjected before things could get heated. "As far as you're concerned, John, the plan remains the same. Got it? Imagine Jock here is Daniel, and Daniel is Malcolm."

"Easy done," John said.

"Jock, you wanna come over here and introduce yerself or are you just gonna stand in the corner and glower?"

Jock pushed himself off the wall, stepped between the sofa and chairs.

"That's a good lad," Steven said. "Now you can stand in the centre of the room and glower."

John stood, offered his hand. They shook. Jock's grip was firm, strong. His face looked one tic away from a sneer.

"Jock yer actual name," John said, "or just a clever nickname cos of yer nationality?" He broke the handshake.

"It's ma name," Jock said. His voice sounded like gravel and crushed glass.

"That's unfortunate."

"At least it's no as fuckin borin as *John*."

"Got us there. At least you haven't got wild ginger hair and yer not wearin a fuckin skirt." Jock's eyes blazed, but before he could say anything John continued. "What were you down in Newcastle for, Jock?"

"None of your fuckin business, pal."

"Aye, probably not. How'd you know Malcolm, then?"

Jock looked past John, at Malcolm.

"We just go back a while, is all," Malcolm said. "Few favours each way here and there."

"All right, all right, that's enough pleasantries," Steven said.

John sat back down.

Daniel was staring at him. "Do you have to antagonise everyone you meet?"

"I don't do it on purpose. It's just part of me charm."

"D'you even know what charm means?"

"Ladies seem to like it." John winked at him. Could see how it irked him, and he didn't even know the half of it. He turned to Jock. "Which part of Scotland are you from, Jock?"

"You ask too many questions, pal," Jock said. He left the centre of the room, returned to the corner.

John turned back to Daniel. "See what happens when I try to be friendly?"

Steven shook his head, pushed himself up from his chair. "I'll give wor lass a shout, tell her to get the brews on."

Chapter Six

The armoured truck made its collection from the bank ten a.m. on Fridays. Daniel parked the van down the road at quarter to. The back of the van faced the front of the bank.

John and Jock were in the van, wearing balaclavas and carrying sawn-off shotguns, waiting. They stayed low. The windows in the back doors had not been blacked out so as not to arouse suspicion. Daniel kept his eyes on the mirrors, ready to give them the go ahead.

Steven had had guys watch the bank. Keep notes. Pass them on to him. Got to know the schedule. He'd planned. Prepared. Set up the job.

In the van, no one spoke. They'd check the time. John wanted to light a cigarette, but he couldn't distract himself, couldn't distract the others. He was on a job. He was a professional.

"Truck's here," Daniel said.

John felt Jock tense up beside him. His grip tightened on the gun. He rolled his shoulders, popped his neck.

John didn't need that. He was already loose. Ready to go at a moment's notice, always.

"Be ready," Daniel said, but neither of them needed to be told. "Bloke's inside." He narrated what he could see. "All right, all right. Get ready to move. Any fuckin second now."

While the guy was inside the bank was the hard part. They were working blind. The person handing over the cash could be slow. Inept. Or it could be a pretty young teller, and the guy was trying to chat her up. To get her number. Maybe she was flirting back. That would add on some extra minutes. Maybe she wasn't interested at all but he was persistent.

Jock growled. "Fucker's been in there a while."

Daniel never looked away from the mirror. "This is standard," he said. "Just be ready."

They were at the back door, coiled to burst out on Daniel's say-so.

Daniel cleared his throat. Jock flinched at the sound like it was the order. He was on edge. Amped up. John could feel the expectancy coming off him. He was raring to go.

Daniel stiffened in his seat, leaned forward. "Door's open," he said. "That's him—*go, go, go.*"

John and Jock kicked open the back doors of the van, burst out and raced for the truck.

Newcastle wasn't busy, but it wasn't quiet, either. There were people on the paths. There were cars on the road. Someone cried out. A couple of people ran at the sight of the masked men with the guns.

Jock went straight to the man carrying the box of money. "On the ground!" His voice was terrifying. So loud it was hard to tell his accent was Scottish. "On the fuckin ground, now!" He waved the shotgun at the man.

John went to the truck's driver, trained his shotgun on the door in case he tried to get out. He didn't. His eyes were wide. He raised his hands in surrender, to show he wasn't going to try anything.

Jock's man raised his hands, too. Got down on his knees.

Jock didn't stop waving the gun. "On yer face! Kiss the fuckin floor!"

John thought he was too loud—the shotgun did more than enough talking—but the man was complying. He pressed his face to the floor. Jock grabbed the box. The man looked up. Jock caught sight of him looking. He kicked him in the side of the face. John saw blood fly, heard something crunch. Someone nearby screamed. Jock was already heading back to the van. John followed him. Daniel had the engine running. They dived inside, slammed the doors. Daniel drove, tore through the streets. No one tried to stop him. No sight or sound of police.

John and Jock tore off the masks, put them and the guns inside a duffel bag, stashed it in a compartment in the van wall, along with the money box.

Daniel pulled into an underground car park. John and Jock were ready with screwdrivers and number plates. They jumped out. John took the one at the rear, Jock the one at the front. They changed the plates, got back inside. John drove now. Daniel rode in the back, where he couldn't be seen. They left the car park and stuck to the limit. John watched the mirrors, made sure they weren't being followed.

They weren't.

They left the city, went north to Ponteland. They went through fields, to a car parked at the side of a country road, under a tree. Waiting for them.

They grabbed the bag of guns and the box of cash, put them in the boot of the car. They rolled the van into the field, doused the interior with petrol, then set it on fire. In the car, they drove back to Newcastle.

"Why'd you kick that bloke?" Daniel said, driving.

"He was lookin," Jock said.

"How hard did you kick him, like? Looked like you were booting a fuckin football."

Jock shrugged. "Dunno."

"Was he still alive?"

Jock shrugged again. "Dinnae care."

John sat in the back. He wound down the window, lit a cigarette.

Chapter Seven

The money box was with Steven. He'd get it open, deal out the shares.

Daniel and Jock had dropped John off, continued on to see the Top Man. John called Mary. Took her a while to answer. He was about to give up, put the phone down. She wasn't as pleased to hear from him as he'd expected. "You don't wanna come round, like?"

"I can't," she said. "Daniel—he might come back."

"He'll be gone for a while yet. Gone to see yer dad. They'll probably gan for a pint after, to celebrate. Meet up with Malcolm, let him know how it all went."

"Ye can't guarantee that, though," she said.

"I nearly can."

"No, you can't. He might come back any time, and I'll not be here."

"So you'll tell him you've been to see a mate. Isn't that what you telt me yer excuse was?"

"I'll be cutting it fine."

John paused a moment. "You looking to put an end to this? That's the case, just say so."

She paused in turn. "No, it's not that."

"Then I don't get why you're bein so reluctant. Are you ill?"

"No, I'm not ill." She fell silent for a while. John waited. She didn't say anything. He began to wonder if the line had died, then he heard her breathe. "Do you love me?"

The question caught him off guard. He gritted his teeth.

"Are you there?"

"Aye."

"Did you hear me?"

"Aye."

"Well?"

"Well what?"

"Are you gonna answer me question, or not? Although, to be honest, sounds like you've already answered it. Now, why're *you* so reluctant?"

"You know what this is. It doesn't exactly have a future, does it?"

She fell silent again. He waited for her to hang up, but she didn't. "What're you scared of?"

"Eh?"

"Are you scared of me dad? I know you're not scared of Daniel."

"I'm not scared of anyone."

"Just scared of commitment then, eh?"

"There's no commitment to be had here. You

already know this. What's the matter with you?"

"Nothing's wrong with me." She took a deep breath. "I can't make it tonight."

The way she'd been talking, John wasn't sure if he'd still wanted her to come round anyway. Didn't want her asking such questions in person, face to face. "All right," he said.

"Aye." Another moment of silence, then the phone died.

John put down the receiver. His eyes narrowed, confused by it all. The call hadn't gone anything like he'd expected it to, and already it began to feel like a dream. Like it had never really happened. He stared at the phone like he expected it to start ringing again, but it didn't.

Chapter Eight

John killed time for a couple of days, waited for a call to tell him his cut was ready.

He paced the floors, did push-ups, sit-ups. Sat by the window and smoked, watched the world go by below. Started to feel stir crazy but wouldn't go out. Didn't want to miss the call.

These were the times, after a job when the cut wasn't immediate and he had to wait for it, that he wished he had a television, or a radio. Hell, even a book. Something to pass the time.

More push-ups. More sit-ups. A little shadow boxing, remembering the training of his youth.

Waiting for the call.

Waiting.

The third day came. Sure this had to be the one. Anything more than three days and it was starting to feel like a piss take.

John sat by the window, smoked his way through a pack, callisthenics forgotten. He ran out of cigarettes. His temper flared. No one rang.

CUTTHROAT

At the end of the third day, there was still no call.

Chapter Nine

John went to the pub, found Malcolm. He was with a woman. Figured it was Tina. She had long blonde hair, tightly curled. Her make-up was heavy, the black around her eyes thick. Her top teeth poked out of her closed mouth, pressing down on her bottom lip. John joined them at their table. Malcolm spun on him, surprised. He realised who it was. "John, Jesus, you gave me a shock there, mate."

"Where's me cut," John said.

"Whoa, lad. Keep yer voice down."

John stared at him. His arm was still bandaged.

Tina looked between the two of them, an eyebrow arched. "Who's this, Malc?" When she opened her mouth, her teeth looked even worse. John remembered Malcolm describing them as being a 'mess'. He wasn't wrong.

"This is me mate, John."

"Isn't he the one you were with when you got cut?"

"That's me," John said. His eyes never left Malcolm. "Answer me question."

"Whey, I dunno why you're askin me, John. Should you not go see the Top Man?"

"I've been. No one home."

"Oh. How'd you know where to find me?"

"I've been looking for a while."

"Ah, so this wasn't a lucky first guess, eh?" He grinned.

John did not. John glared. "Are you gonna answer me fuckin question, or what?"

"Jesus, Malc," Tina said. "He's tightly wound, isn't he?"

John ignored her. Malcolm did, too. "You haven't heard anything yet, like?" Malcolm said.

"Oh aye, I've heard somethin, that's why I've been out looking all round town for you to ask where me fuckin cut is. Get a fuckin clue, man."

"All right, all right, calm down. Sorry, man. I thought someone would've given you a call."

"No one's called. I've been sitting on me fuckin hands for the last three days, man."

"Jesus, sorry, John. Uh, so basically, the money's not ready yet."

John didn't like that. He leaned forward. "You wanna run that by me again?"

"Like I said. It's not ready yet. Sorry."

John felt his fists clench, his teeth grind. Before anyone knew what he was doing, he'd reached across the table, grabbed Malcolm by his bandaged arm, squeezed and twisted.

"*Fuck*!" Malcolm's body contorted, he bit his lip.

"Jesus fuckin Christ, man! Get off us!"

Red appeared on the bandage, the wound reopened. John didn't let go.

"Here, man!" Tina said. "What're you doin, man? Get off him!" She was loud. Probably drawing attention to them all.

"Piss off, pet," John said. "He's a big lad. He can take it." John shot her a look, shut her up. She backed down, but she continued to stare.

Malcolm gasped for breath. "John, John, please," he said, begging off. "Let go of me arm, man, *please*. Let us explain."

John held it firm. He squeezed a little more, a gasp escaped Malcolm, then he let go. Blood was leaking through the bandage. A drop hit the table between them. Malcolm held the arm to himself, cradled it by the elbow.

Tina leaned over, inspected it. "Look what you've done man, you fuckin arsehole. He's gonna have to get that stitched back up."

"Pet, sit down and fuckin shut up. I don't care. I'll tear his fuckin arm off and beat the two of you with it if he doesn't hurry up and give us a decent explanation."

"You've got some mouth on you," she said. "You wanna—"

"Tina, *please*," Malcolm said.

She looked between them, ran her tongue round the inside of her mouth. "Talk it out between yerselves, then. I'm goin for a piss, and I hope you're gone when I get back." She stood. Her dress was short. John caught a glimpse of her legs out the corner of his eye, remembered what Malcolm had said about them. His nickname for her. He wasn't impressed.

She squeezed by, headed off to the toilets. John didn't watch her go. Had eyes now only for Malcolm. "Spit it out," he said.

"It's just taking the Top Man a bit longer to get the cash clean, that's all," Malcolm said, his voice earnest, desperate to be believed and not be hurt again.

"You having a laugh?"

"I swear down, mate. *Swear down*. It was a hot job, it's just taking a bit longer than he thought it would, that's all. He'll be in touch with you soon as it's ready."

"I want paid," John said. "Tell that fat cunt to get me fuckin money by Friday. I divvint care if it has to come out of his own pocket, I want me cut."

Malcolm nodded. "Yeah, yeah, of course. I'll pass it on, mate."

"Until I've got me cut, divvint call us mate, Malcolm," John said. He tapped the table twice. "Get me fuckin money, or I'm gonna be pissed."

He stood, left. Passed Tina on his way out. She must've seen something in his face. She didn't have anything smart to say. She stayed clear of him.

Chapter Ten

John didn't pass the time locked away in his flat. He went out. If he missed a call, they'd call again. He'd sent a message. He was serious. They didn't want to piss him off.

Thursday came. It started to snow. He stayed inside that day. Out the cold, although his flat wasn't much warmer. He watched the snow fall. Cars crawled by on the roads below, careful on the corners. He heard a lot of skidding, a lot of horns blaring. It got dark early. He could see his breath in front of his face. He sat on his sofa, wrapped in his coat, his arms folded. The snow had stopped, but that didn't help anything. John was steadfast. Wouldn't be moved by the cold. Wouldn't allow himself to shiver. He gritted his teeth and toughed it out, stared at the phone like he could will it into action.

It didn't ring.

He could feel his temper boiling over. It shouldn't have taken this long. They were leaving it to the last minute. Taking the piss. Mocking him.

The phone rang. John answered. It wasn't Steven. It wasn't Malcolm, or Daniel.

It was Mary.

"I'm surprised to hear from you," John said.

"Are you expecting someone else?"

"Aye, actually. I am."

"Oh. Well, don't let me keep you."

"I can spare a couple of minutes. They'll call back. What do you want?"

"To apologise for the last time we talked. I don't know what came over me. I'm sorry we didn't meet up."

"It was a shame."

"I'm free now."

John took his time answering. Let her wait. "All right."

"I'll come to you."

"Aye."

They both hung up. John put the phone down. If they still hadn't called by the time Mary arrived, at least he'd have a more enjoyable way to pass the time.

Mary knocked on his door. There hadn't been a call in the meantime. "You were fast," John said, letting her in.

She shrugged. "Bus must've been on time. Do you wanna talk about my timekeeping or would you rather do something else?"

"Suppose we'd better get to something else before you change your mind."

"Change my mind?"

53

"Like the other night."

"I already said sorry for that. Let's not keep going on about it."

"Where's Daniel tonight, then?"

"Out. Like, outside of Newcastle. He didn't tell me where."

John frowned. "Out of Newcastle?"

"Just for the night."

"And he didn't tell you where?"

"It's not the first time."

"That doesn't bother you?"

"Why do you wanna keep talking about my husband?" She grabbed him by the hand, led him through to the bedroom. "Come on. I didn't come here to talk."

John let her lead. In the bedroom she got straight to work. She took off her clothes, then removed his. Pushed him back onto the bed then climbed on top. John held her by the waist, let her do the work. He kept one ear on her heavy breaths, the other on the phone.

It didn't ring.

He watched her face. There was something different there, he couldn't put his finger on it. Like she was distracted, almost. Her head was turned to the side. Her eyes were narrowed. She was thinking, lost in her mind. John thought, too. Thought back. All the other times she'd been on top. She'd throw her head back, she'd gasp and giggle, she'd chew her lip. Her eyes would close, or they would look straight into his. She was never distracted.

"You all right?"

She snapped back to attention, startled. "I'm fine," she said. And she smiled. She was into it, in the moment, like her old self. John wondered if it was forced.

Mary made extra effort. She bit his shoulder, clawed his chest. John grabbed her by the hair at the back of her head, kissed her. Forced or not, they were having fun now. He flipped her over, got on top. Squeezed her buttocks. He finished and fell to the side.

Mary shivered. "Do you not have heating, man?"

"What're you talking about," John said, trying to catch his breath. "That warmed the room right up."

"For you, maybe. I'm still freezing, man."

"Get under the blanket."

"Just pass me clothes."

John did as she said. Mary rolled off the bed, got to her feet, started dressing. She continued to shiver as she did so. "It's so cold in here," she said. "How do you stand it?"

"Keeps me tough."

"It'll make you ill."

"I've been fine so far."

"Then maybe I'm just soft."

"You feel firm to me."

She shook her hips a little, then pulled on her dress. "Okay," she said. "I'm gonna go."

"So soon?" John cocked his head. "What's your

rush? I thought Daniel was gone all night."

"He is, but I want to sleep in my bed, a comfortable bed, not that rickety old thing you're lying on."

"Nowt wrong with it." John shook his body, the bedsprings squeaked in protest.

"And it's too cold in here. I want some heat."

"Suit yourself." John rolled off the bed, pulled on his pants, walked her to the door.

Mary left, but she paused out in the hallway, turned back to him. Stepped closer. There was an odd look in her eyes, a kind of sadness.

Despite her apparent earlier distraction, this still caught John by surprise. "What's wrong?"

She forced a smile. "Nothing," she said. "Just realised I hadn't said bye." She leaned up closer to his face, kissed him. "Bye." She turned, left.

John watched her disappear down the hall, then closed the door. The look on her face had thrown him. The quickness of her visit had thrown him. He went to the window, watched the street below, watched her walk away. Saw her footprints in the snow as she crossed the road. Remembered what she'd said about the bus running on time. Thought it strange that the buses were running at all in such weather.

He put a cigarette in his mouth, but before he could light it, the phone rang. Malcolm. "All right, mate?"

"I'm fine," John said. "What do you want?"

"Well, what do you think I want? I thought you'd be glad to hear from us."

"I'd have been gladder to hear sooner."

"Aye, well, I told you it was taking some time. Anyway, it's all sorted now. You wanna come over and pick it up?"

"Aye."

"Canny. We'll see you soon then, eh?"

"Where?"

"Eh?"

"Where are you?"

"What? Oh. I'm at the Top Man's house."

"So he came back, did he?"

"He said you must've just missed him the other day. They'd only gone to the shops."

John grunted. "Mm. Aye, I'll be there soon."

"Canny."

John put the phone down, went through to the bedroom and pulled his shirt back on. He laced up his shoes and put on a coat then headed out into the night.

Outside, his breath misted thicker than it had in the flat. It was cold, bitterly so. It bit at his face, at all the exposed areas of his skin. He shoved his hands into his pockets, walked fast to keep the blood pumping.

He reached the corner at the end of the street and felt strong hands grab him from behind. He nearly lost his footing, slipping in the slush underfoot, but he managed to keep himself upright. The frozen path slowed his movements. He felt himself punched in the back of the head before he could start grabbing and swinging, then he was dragged down an alley, thrown up against the wall. The air was forced from his lungs by the impact. Another fist caught him in the stomach, winded him further.

Doubled-up, he was hauled from the wall, held from behind. The grip was strong. Too strong to break in his weakened, dazed state.

He realised then that there wasn't just one attacker. There were two. He counted four legs.

Something pressed to his throat. Slid. Warmth spilled down his front. He tasted blood, a lot of it.

A voice spoke into his ear, breath tingling on his lobe. "Fuck you, ye dirty fuckin cunt." The voice was familiar but too much was happening, he couldn't place it.

He was shoved onto the cold ground. He gasped for breath. His blood poured into the virgin white snow, coloured it red. Bright red. John felt himself hypnotised by the colour.

His attackers were still present. Looming over him. Watching him bleed. Watching him die. John forced himself to turn. To look up. See who had done this to him.

Both were familiar to him. The voice struck home. Daniel.

Beside him, Jock.

Daniel still held the bloodied knife. He wiped the blade on the snow, pocketed it. He spat on John. The two of them turned, left the alley, hurried away from the scene.

John gasped for breath. Tried to push himself up, the cold biting into his hands as they curled at the ground, sought purchase.

His vision began to blur. To darken at the edges.

Part Two
Newcastle
1976 to 1978

Chapter Eleven

Mary wore white, but she hadn't been a virgin for a very long time.

Daniel wore a navy blue pinstripe suit. He usually dressed smart, but for his wedding day, he'd made an extra effort. He'd joked to her beforehand that he was going to grow a moustache to look extra refined for the big day.

"Nah, yer not," Mary said.

"Why aye, man." Daniel stroked his top lip. "I'll look amazing with a moustache. Can't you picture it?"

"I can't picture you with any facial hair. And especially not a bloody moustache."

"Me dad had a moustache."

"You don't look anything like your dad did, though. You look like your mother. And *she* certainly doesn't have a moustache."

"*Her* mam does."

"Daniel, man! I'm serious. I divvint want a lifetime looking at wedding photographs and you've got this unsightly fuckin face fuzz on yer top lip."

The day rolled round and she was pleased to see he remained clean-shaven. He could see the relief on her face when she got to the front of the church, escorted by her father. He grinned, winked at her.

She'd met Daniel two years before, when he first started working for her dad. He'd been a runner, doing odd jobs here and there. It brought him up to the house a lot. They got to talk. To flirt. Daniel was careful around her father. Tried to avoid being seen talking to her when he was around.

Eventually he worked up the nerve to ask Steven if it was all right to take his daughter out on a date.

"You gonna be a gentleman?"

"Well, aye, of course."

"Sounds like she's in for a boring night, then." He'd winked.

Daniel had told her the story afterward. Mary shook her head, rolled her eyes. "I reckon he thinks he can embarrass me, but he can't. And if he's not trying to embarrass me, well, that's just disgusting."

As it transpired, Daniel wasn't a gentleman on that first date. They went out to dinner and he stroked her leg under the table. Drew circles on her knee, ran his fingers higher so they were under the hem of her dress, high up on the inside of her thigh.

"Is this you on your best behaviour?" Mary said, raising an eyebrow.

"You haven't seen the best of me yet." Daniel grinned.

"That was a terribly cheesy line."

"Those are my moves—I make you laugh now, I'll make you gasp later."

Mary did laugh. She laughed hard. She shook her head and said, "You wanker."

But later, he did make her gasp. Took her back to his place in Benwell and straight to his bedroom. In the back of the taxi on the way over, they'd been all over each other, hands and mouths, his fingers slipping further and further up her dress until they were inside her underwear, inside her.

So no, Mary wasn't a virgin, Daniel wasn't even her first, second, third, or fourth, but still she wore white and she looked beautiful.

On the morning of Mary's wedding, while she dressed, her mother had had tears in her eyes. "Look at you, pet," she'd said, wiping the streaks from her cheek. "You're radiant, man. Wait til yer dad sees you."

"Mam, stop crying, man," Mary said. "You're gonna ruin your make-up."

Her mother cried during the ceremony. Mary could hear her sniffling all the way through. Daniel could hear it, too. They exchanged glances while the priest ran through his lines, tried not to giggle at each other.

After, her mother was quick to gush over Daniel, too. "Ye look so handsome, Daniel," she said, still crying. She blew her nose, stuffed the tissue back down her sleeve, readjusted her hat to get up on her tiptoes and kiss him on the cheek. She sniffed. "The two of you, what a pair. Just imagine what the kids will look like." She patted Mary on the stomach as if she were already pregnant.

Mary brushed her hand off. "Mam, man—slow down."

Steven put his arm around Denise's shoulders. "Aye, save that kind of talk for after the wedding night at least, eh?" He nudged Daniel.

Mary covered her face, shook her head.

Malcolm walked over, joined them. "The photographer wants to get some pictures of the best man with the main man," he said. He leaned past Daniel, kissed Mary on the cheek. "You look fuckin *stunning* Mary, pet. Far too good for the likes of this one."

"Who's she gonna get that's better, eh?" Daniel said.

"Could you not have cut your hair for today, Malcolm?" Denise said.

"What's wrong with me hair?" Malcolm said. "It's luscious. Are you jealous of it or somethin, Denise?"

"You look like a bloody hippy, man," Steven said, laughing. "Yer ten years out of date."

"That's nothing," Mary said. "Daniel was talking about growing a moustache."

Denise's eyes went wide. "Well I'm glad you saw sense, Daniel."

"Decided Malcolm had enough hair for the both of us," Daniel said.

Malcolm stroked his own moustache. "That's true. Still, I reckon you'd be improved by a tash."

"That's what I said."

"I disagreed," Mary said. "Still do."

"One day," Daniel said to Malcolm. They grinned.

"Didn't the photographer want you both?" Mary said.

The two of them went off and Mary was left alone with her parents. "Suppose we'd better go talk to Daniel's mam for a bit," Steven said. "You all right, pet?"

"Yeah, I'm fine." She smiled.

"We'll get wrapped up here then get along to the club," he said. "Get a few pints in us, have a good time."

"Get you off them heels," Denise said. "You can relax, really enjoy yourself now."

Mary didn't get to relax at the club. She spent the night after the wedding breakfast going from table to table, talking with friends and family, seeing how everyone was doing, making sure they were enjoying themselves. Daniel spent most of his time sitting with Malcolm and his other friends, getting drunk. She took him to one side when she got a chance.

"Do you not wanna come round with me?" she said. "Say hello to everyone?"

"You're doin a good enough job on yer own, pet," he said, squeezing her shoulder and planting a sloppy kiss on her forehead. He was already drunk, swaying where he stood. His cheeks were flushed and his eyes were half-closed. Mary left him to it, continued doing her rounds.

She remembered when he proposed. Took her back to the restaurant where they had their first date. Kept his hands to himself this time, fidgeted and seemed nervous. She'd already worked out what he was going to ask her. Daniel never got nervous, and it wasn't like he was going to break up with her. They hadn't been having any problems, and he was probably too scared of her father, and losing everything he'd earned working for him. Not that she wanted him to stay with her through fear, but it was another reason she knew they weren't heading for a break-up and he was more likely to propose.

Mary was an only child, and it had looked likely for a while that Steven was grooming Daniel to take over from him. Now that he was married in, part of the family, his position was assured.

They stayed at the club until after midnight. People trailed off in taxis and a minibus. Mary was saying goodbye to her parents, only a few stragglers remaining in the club and getting glared at by the bar staff who wanted to go home. Most of those who remained were Daniel's friends. They were drunk and loud. A glass fell from the table, smashed as it hit the ground. They all laughed.

"Well, have fun clearing them out," Denise said, kissing her daughter on the cheek.

Steven hugged Mary. "Enjoy the rest of your night," he said. "Have a nice lie-in tomorrow, eh?"

Her parents left and Mary heard Daniel call to her from across the room. "Wife! Wife, get over here and sit with us!"

Mary rolled her eyes, went to them. Daniel pulled her onto his lap. "Think we should be getting home soon?" Mary said.

Daniel wriggled his eyebrows. "Oh, why aye. I get ye."

They cleared out the club and got a taxi home. A new house in Jesmond that her father had bought for them as a wedding gift. "I'd carry ye over the threshold," Daniel said, "but I might drop ye."

"I wouldn't let ye," she said. "At this rate, I'm gonna have to carry *you* over it."

They propped each other up and walked in together. Daniel had had a lot to drink, he was unsteady and used the wall for support. He took a deep breath, shook his head, straightened up. "I'm fine," he said. "I'm fine. I've still got a job to do." He smirked.

He stank like a distillery, but still had only one thing on his mind. Mary only had a couple of glasses of wine, still felt sober. "C'mon then," she said, taking him by the hand and leading him upstairs. "Let's get this over with. I'm bloody knackered and ready for bed now."

Before they were fully through the bedroom door, Daniel was already tearing at her dress.

"Calm down, man," she said. "You're gonna rip it."

"Whey, we're not gonna need it again," he said.

"Here, just calm down." Mary pushed him onto the bed so he was sitting. She took off the dress while he removed his clothes. He didn't seem as drunk as before, now. He was focused. Lust had sobered him somewhat. He got his clothes off and watched her. Licked his lips. Started playing with himself.

"C'mon, pet," he said. "I'll be done before we start at this rate."

Mary grabbed him by the wrist. "Slow down, then," she said.

She was naked, she climbed on top, gripped him, started to slide him inside.

Daniel put his hands on her buttocks, held her in place. "Uh-uh," he said. He spun, threw her onto the bed. "We've done all this before," he said, crawling up her. He put his hand between her legs. "It's our wedding night. We need to do something special. Something you've never done before." His fingers probed lower, beyond her vagina, between her butt cheeks.

"Whoa, hang on," Mary said, squirming up the bed away from him. "Nah, calm down. You're not putting it up me arse."

"Howay, you wore white. We might as well do your only virgin hole left." He nuzzled her neck. His fingers were persistent. Mary could feel them circling. Daniel chewed on her ear lobe, stuck his tongue into it. His other hand grabbed her breast, pinned her to the bed by it.

"Daniel, man. You're being too rough."

He stuck his tongue into her mouth, like he was trying to shut her up. Mary reached between his legs, took hold of him, tried to guide him in to take his mind off his thoughts of anal action, make him forget. The tip prised open her lips.

"No," Daniel said, pushing himself up. "I told you what I want."

Mary opened her mouth, but before she could say anything he flipped her over onto her front. She felt and heard him draw himself up onto his knees. Mary tried to turn. Daniel put a hand flat on her back, kept her in place. "What're you doin, man?" she said.

"Just relax," he said. "It's fine. You'll like it. Just stay still, will ye."

He sucked a finger, got it wet, pushed it in. Mary's body went stiff. She grabbed handfuls of the blanket in both fists. Daniel worked his finger in and out, up to the knuckle. "There we go," he said. He was breathing hard, almost panting. "There we go, nearly there."

Mary felt him move again, slide his finger out and grip her hips with both hands. He spread her legs, raised her a little. He forced his way in. Mary cried out. She bit into the pillow. Daniel groaned, long and low.

"Just calm down," he said. "Just relax. You're making this harder than it needs to be."

Mary tried to relax, to go limp, but it hurt. Daniel began to thrust. It felt like he was going to split her. She felt like she was bleeding.

Daniel stroked the side of her face. "That's my girl," he said. "Just relax."

Chapter Twelve

Mary and Daniel had been married for a year and a half when she first met John properly. She'd seen him a couple of times at her parents' house, talking to her father or her husband, but she'd never spoken to him herself. She'd noticed him looking at her, though. Studying the side of her face from afar. A casual glance at her behind as she passed by.

It was her father's birthday party. They were in the same club where Mary and Daniel had celebrated their wedding. In a repeat of that night, Daniel was sitting with his friends, getting drunk. Mary was on her own, sipping a wine in the corner of the room. She didn't much feel like socialising. Rarely did. Not those days. She was in mourning.

Denise joined her daughter on her way back from the bar, carrying a wine for herself and another pint for her husband. "What're you doing all alone?" she said.

"I'm not feeling great," Mary said. It wasn't a total lie.

"Oh?" Denise pressed the back of her hand to Mary's forehead.

"It's not a temperature," Mary said. "Just stomach stuff."

"Why isn't Daniel sitting with you?"

"He's getting drunk. I don't mind, mam. We all deal with things in our own way."

"Mm." Denise looked towards Daniel and his table. He was laughing. It wasn't the best time for her to look over. Seemed like Malcolm had said something funny. "He should sit with you. He doesn't look like he even bloody cares."

"He cares." Mary nodded. "He does care."

"He's got a funny way of showing it."

Mary took a drink. "Why don't you go sit with Dad, mam? He'll be wondering where his pint is. I'm all right. How's he enjoying his birthday, anyway?"

"He's having a good time. He's canny drunk, planning on getting drunker." She tapped the side of the fresh drink she'd got for him.

"Where is he? I've barely seen him."

"Over there, at the back of that big group there," Denise said. "All the hangers-on swarming round him, showering him with gifts he doesn't need. Do you wanna come over and see him?"

"I saw him when I got here, I'll let him enjoy his night. Go sit with him, mam, he'd like you to be there. He needs someone genuine by his side when he's surrounded by all those sycophants."

"If you're sure you're all right."

"I'm sure, mam. I'm happy." She held up her wine, forced a smile.

Denise leaned in, kissed her on the cheek. "You'll get more chances, pet. Divvint you worry. You're still young." She kissed her again, then disappeared into the gathering of people.

Mary felt a stab in her heart, a twinge at the back of her throat like she was about to start crying. She swallowed it down, pressed a hand to her stomach. She realised what she was doing and took her hand away, laid it flat on the tabletop. There was nothing there. Nothing inside.

She'd had a miscarriage. It had been a month since it happened, since she'd woken up to find her bed-sheets stained red, blood pouring down her legs and a painful cramp in her womb like the onset of a period.

Daniel didn't take the news well.

Of course he was panicked in the morning, waking up to see all the blood, to find it all over his own legs as well as hers. He'd rushed her to the hospital. He was crushed by the news of the miscarriage, though he'd refrained from shedding any tears. Mary had not. She'd cried herself dry, night after night, for more than a week.

Daniel dealt with his grief in another way. Threw himself into the company of his friends. Got drunk every night. On the nights he did come home, he slept downstairs, on the sofa. There was a growing distance between them. Daniel became cold.

Mary woke him on the sofa one morning. He

rolled his head to see her, looked at her through the half-closed eyes of a hangover headache. He smacked his dry lips, white at the corners of his mouth. He ran the back of his hand over his jaw, his knuckles scraping on stubble. The shirt he'd gone out in was unbuttoned all the way down. His stomach protruded over his belt buckle, filled with beer. He stunk of alcohol and sweat. The stench had been soaking into the sofa. Mary had caught its whiff when she sat there a few days before.

"What?" Daniel said.

"We need to talk."

He pushed himself up to a sitting position, pressed a hand to his forehead, groaned. "Right now?"

"Aye, I think so."

He took a deep breath. "Get on with it then."

"We need to talk about the miscarriage."

"What's there to talk about? It happened."

"I feel like you blame me for it."

He looked at her. "Whey, I wasn't the one carrying our bairn, was I?"

Mary's breath caught. She forced herself not to cry. "It wasn't my fault, Daniel. There was nothing I could've done to stop it. These things happen. There's nothing anyone could've done."

"Mm."

"You sound like you don't believe me."

"Our baby's dead."

"That's a dagger through my heart, Daniel. Please don't say that to me. Please don't say it ever again."

Daniel stared at her.

"*Please.*"

"All right." He pushed himself up off the sofa. "I'm goin for a bath." He stumbled out the room, up the stairs.

Their little talk hadn't resolved anything. Daniel remained distant. If anything, he got colder.

One night, Mary was still downstairs when he got home. Drunk, of course. "You still up?" he said.

"Couldn't sleep."

"Feeling better then, are you?"

"Yeah, a bit."

"You've been in bed a lot since the miscarriage."

"I know I have." It wasn't through any pain or illness. She was depressed. She couldn't bring herself to get out of bed. Couldn't bring herself to tackle the day. Talking to her angry husband was as much energy as she could muster. "How much longer is this going to go on for, Daniel?"

"How long's *what* gonna go on for?"

"*This.* Going out every bloody night, getting drunk. Not talking to me, avoiding me, and when I do manage to corner you like this, you're standoffish. You're angry at me so much, and I can't understand why."

"You don't know *why*?"

"But that wasn't my fault!"

Daniel stopped himself from saying anything further. He took a deep breath in through his nose. "If you don't wanna stay on the settee, you'd better gan upstairs now cos I wanna get some kip." He turned like he was heading to the kitchen.

Mary stopped him. "Daniel, this doesn't have to be the end."

Daniel stopped, turned back. "The end of what?"

"Of the baby conversation."

"There is no baby."

"I know that—that's not what I mean. I mean another baby. More babies. There's no reason why we can't try again. There's nothing stopping us."

Daniel's face turned. It shocked her. He looked angry. But more than that—he looked disgusted, too. "Nowt stopping us? You think I wanna gan through *this* again?"

"It'll be different next time—"

"How can it be different? You said it wasn't your fault. If it wasn't your fault, how can you stop it from happening again? Or was that just a lie? Maybe it was your fault and you just won't admit it."

Mary felt her eyes burning. She shook her head.

Daniel walked towards her. Mary flinched. Daniel got close. "You can't even grow a baby right, man— what fuckin good are you?" He looked her up and down, sneered, turned and went upstairs, to the bedroom. He slammed the door. Mary remained where she was. She wouldn't let herself cry.

Looking at her husband, across the room at her father's birthday party, she remembered that night. Remembered all the nights. He hadn't touched her since the miscarriage. She suspected other women weren't treated this way.

She watched her husband and told herself she would not cry.

"Isn't this your dad's birthday party?"

Mary looked up. It was John, though she didn't know his name at the time. "Aye," she said. She cleared her throat.

"Then how come you're sitting alone?"

She shrugged. "Just how I fancied it. I've seen you around."

"Aye, likewise. John." He offered his hand. Mary shook it, gave her name. He carried a pint, put it on the table and joined her. "You mind me sitting? I won't take up too much of yer time, if you don't want us to."

"I don't mind. You're not going to go schmooze?" She indicated the corner where her father sat, and all the people gathered round him.

"Christ, no. I got an invite, I turned up. I've fulfilled any obligation I might've had. I'm not gonna go over there and embarrass meself like the rest of them."

"It *is* disgusting, isn't it?"

"So how come you're alone? Yer husband's just over there."

"I don't have to be with him at all times."

"Just looked a bit lonely over here is all."

"That why you came and sat with me?"

"Aye." He took a drink. "That's why."

Chapter Thirteen

The first time they met was at the Monument. Mary got the bus into the city, walked there to find him. John sat on the steps. He wouldn't give her his home address. As she approached him he looked beyond her, checking to see if she was being followed, to make sure she'd come alone.

He stood. "Pleasant trip?"

"It was the bus," she said. "What d'you think?"

"Whey, when they finish building this Metro they keep banging on about, it won't take so long."

"Still be full of rowdy Geordies, though."

"Not so bad if you know how to handle them."

"How you handle people is probably different to how I handle them."

John started walking. Mary followed, caught up, walked alongside him. "You wanna go anywhere first?" he said. "You hungry?"

"No, I'm not hungry."

"All right."

She hesitated, kept step with him. "I've never

done this kind of thing before."

John said nothing.

"Have you?"

"I've never been married."

"That's not what I mean."

"Then what do you mean?"

Mary looked round, made sure there was no one close enough to hear. "Meeting up with a married woman in the middle of the day while her husband is away."

"That's quite specific."

"You know what I mean."

John grunted, but he didn't answer her question.

Mary was going to press him for one but he started crossing a road. It was busy and she quickened her pace to avoid being hit by the passing cars. "Jesus Christ, John—slow down!"

"If I slow down we'll get hit." They reached the other side.

"Give me a little warning next time, then."

"I saw an opening."

They were away from the city centre, off the busy roads and travelling through quieter ones, down residential streets.

"Reckon you'll remember the way?" he said.

"Who's to say this isn't just a one-time thing?"

"I suppose we'll have to wait and see, won't we?" He pointed ahead at a block of flats. "It's that one."

Mary felt a flush of excitement course through her. It was true, she'd never done anything like this before. Now, John's home in sight, she had butterflies. Her cheeks were tingling. Her nerves were on edge, but not in a bad way. She felt like she had when she was younger, when she still lived at home with her parents, and she'd sneak out to visit boyfriends they didn't know she had. It was the same kind of feeling.

John led her inside, up the stairs to his home. Held the door open for her to enter first. "I'd give you the grand tour," he said, "but there's nothing grand about it. You can pretty much see it all already."

Mary looked round. "Bit of a dump, isn't it?" It didn't abate her excitement any, however. If anything, it spiked it a little.

"I'm hurt," John said. "I knew I'd have company so I cleaned especially. Can't you tell?" He took off his jacket, hung it on the back of the door.

"I'd hate to have seen what it looked like before you gave it a once over."

John stepped closer to her, so close she could feel his breath upon her cheeks. He was taller than her, looking down at her. He took off her coat, lay it down over the arm of the sofa. "Good thing you didn't come here to inspect the cleanliness of the place."

Mary's mouth was dry. She could feel her heart pounding hard. She could feel other things, too. She hadn't been this close to a man for a long time.

John leaned in, kissed her.

Mary almost pulled away.

She remembered Daniel.

Her husband.

There was reluctance in her kiss. John sensed it, pulled back, looked at her, raised an eyebrow. "Do you want to do this?" he said. "There's nothing stopping you from just walking away."

She remembered the miscarriage.

Remembered what Daniel had said to her.

You can't even grow a baby right.

Remembered the blame he had placed upon her for the death of their child.

She put her hands on the side of John's face, moved them to the back of his neck, held him, kissed him hard.

They went to the bedroom.

Chapter Fourteen

Mary and John's clandestine meetings had been going on for four months, and as far as she was aware, Daniel was none the wiser.

He was still out at all hours. Getting drunk or working, or planning for the next job. If it was none of the above, he was likely fucking one of his many whores. Mary had smelt enough perfume on his collar by then to know the facts. She wasn't going to deceive herself, wasn't going to bother trying. Truth was, she didn't care. Not anymore. Let him fuck other women. She was fucking another man.

But then the night came when Daniel was home before her, and he was awaiting her return.

He was in the sitting room, in darkness. The sound of his voice caught her by surprise. "Where've you been?"

She gave a start while hanging up her coat. Turned to see his silhouette backlit by a car's headlights outside passing over the window. As soon as she saw him, she kicked herself. She'd seen John the night before, right before Malcolm got slashed. She should have known two nights in a row was cutting it fine. They'd gotten sloppy. "Jesus Christ, Daniel. You nearly gave me a heart attack there, man. What're you doing lurking in the shadows for?"

"Waiting for you," he said. "You didn't answer me."

Mary busied herself, pretended she hadn't heard. "Answer what?"

"I asked where you've been."

"Oh, y'know, just out."

"It's late."

"I was with friends. We went for a drink, a catch up."

"That right? That sounds nice. Who were you with?"

"Linda." Mary had already run through this conversation in her mind what felt like a thousand times before.

"Linda, eh?"

"Aye."

"How was it?"

"Fine. Nice. You know what Linda's like, though. Talks for England. Couldn't get away. Didn't realise the time, to be honest."

Daniel's voice was low. "I know you weren't with Linda, Mary."

She played innocent. "Eh? What d'you mean?"

"Where were you two weeks ago? Tuesday, I think it was. Were you with Linda, then? What about last night? Linda again?"

The conversation she'd played out in her mind had never gone like this. Mary felt herself losing control of the situation. She hadn't planned it out this far, or for this kind of variable. "No."

"Who, then? Heather? Joanne? Which name do you want to try feeding me this time?"

Mary didn't answer. It felt like the safer option.

"I've noticed you've been going out a lot, Mary. Behind me back. I dunno when it started, but I've been watching you for a month now. Sneaking round, not saying anything about it. And always when I'm out. Always when you think you can beat me back home. Except you didn't. I got back before you, and imagine my surprise to find that you weren't here. I mean, I was *really* surprised. So I went back out and waited in the car. Parked down the road a bit so you wouldn't see me. You didn't get back for another ninety minutes. I was counting. I wanted to ask you where you'd been then, oh believe me, I wanted to ask you—but I thought to myself, no. Let's give her the benefit of the doubt. So I did. But I was always home before you, pet. And I always saw you get back late. And I know you weren't with any of your mates, cos I went by their houses. Checked them out. If they weren't in, if they were with anyone, it was never you."

He fell silent and the two of them looked at each other. The silence drew out. Mary held her breath.

"So, howay," Daniel said. "I'll ask you again, and

this time try givin us the truth, eh? Where've you been?"

It took Mary a long time to answer. She couldn't tell him the truth. She bit her lip. "I've already told you."

Daniel sighed. It was long, exasperated. He got to his feet. "Do you really wanna keep lying to me?"

She stood her ground, braced herself. "I'm not lying."

Daniel went to her. Mary wanted to run, but there was nowhere to go. Upstairs? He would follow. Outside? He would catch her. He was faster.

His hand shot out, grabbed her by the wrist. Yanked on her arm and twisted it, spun her round so her back was to him. He held her in place, his hand around her throat. He pulled up. Mary's back arced. She felt a burn in her shoulder. She gritted her teeth, but a cry escaped her.

"Are you gonna tell me, or do I have to keep hurting you?" Daniel's mouth was close to her ear. "I can hurt you in places it won't show, Mary. No one will know. But you'll know. You'll feel it. Believe me, you'll fucking feel it. For days. And if you still won't tell me, then I'll wait until it doesn't hurt anymore and I'll do it all over again."

Tears ran from Mary's eyes with the pain. She bit her lip. Daniel twisted on her arm a little more. It felt like it was going to pop out of its socket, to tear free of her body. "Okay, okay," Mary gasped. "Just let me go. Please, just let me go…"

Chapter Fifteen

Daniel had never liked John.

He thought he was too cocky. Too arrogant. More than that, he was dangerous. Too dangerous to be around and not have to worry about watching your own back.

And it turned out he'd been fucking his wife.

Mary admitted it and Daniel had to walk away from her. If he hadn't, he wasn't sure what he might have done to her.

Of course, it wasn't as simple as being able to just walk away. He had to make sure she couldn't leave, couldn't let John know that he now knew the truth. He kept hold of her arm but then he grabbed her by the hair, too. Dragged her up the stairs, to their bedroom. A bed they would likely never share again.

He threw her down to the floor, then tore the phone from the wall. Pulled the cable from the plug. Mary tried to beg off. "Daniel, what are you doing? Please, you don't need to do this…"

"Shut up," he said. "I don't want to hear another

fucking word out of you." He grabbed her by the front of her dress, pulled her upright, pushed her onto the bed. He climbed on top of her, pinned her down with a knee either side. Bound her wrists to the headboard. He tied her ankles at the bottom using scarves pulled from her wardrobe. Used another to gag her, to silence any screams she might try to utter.

He left her there, left the house, went to the pub. Planned to get drunk. Didn't know what he'd do when he got home. Didn't know if he'd go home. Maybe he'd go see John...

No, that would be stupid. That would be the worst thing he could do. Facing John head-on, especially with a drink in him, was setting himself up for failure.

Daniel ordered another drink and retreated to a corner of the pub. It was quiet, only a few other men present, and he was glad. No one he knew. He wanted to be left alone. Wanted to drink and get angry. To ask himself, who else knew? *Did* anyone else know?

He doubted it. No one would keep that from him. No one would fucking dare.

He went outside to a payphone. It was cold. He pulled his coat tight around himself while he dialled Malcolm's number. Tina answered. "Malcolm there?"

"Aye, I'll get him for you."

Malcolm came on the line a moment later. "All right, Daniel? What's up?"

Daniel gave him the name of the pub. "Come along. We need to have a drink."

"Uh, okay. Something wrong?"

"Just get along here. Quick as you can. We're gonna talk."

Daniel put the phone down and went back inside. Got another drink, and one for Malcolm when he arrived. He passed the time by dwelling on his anger. Thinking about John fucking his wife. Wondered how many times it had happened. Longer than a month, obviously. He hadn't asked her for details. He didn't want to know. If she'd shared them, she'd likely be dead already.

When Malcolm arrived Daniel was nearly finished his drink and contemplating starting on the one he'd got for Malcolm.

"That for me?" Malcolm planted himself on a stool, took the pint before Daniel answered. Had a long drink. He put the glass back down, smacked his lips, looked at Daniel. Saw the severe expression on his face. Malcolm frowned. "What's the matter with you?"

"Do you know already?"

Malcolm cocked his head. "Know what?"

Daniel stared at him, studied him. "Do you know about Mary?"

"Something happened to Mary?"

"He say anything to you last night, did he? About her?"

"Last night? Who, *John*? About Mary? What're you talkin about?"

Daniel shook his head. "Nah, you don't know. Good."

"I divvint even kna what yer fuckin talkin about, man."

Daniel told him. Malcolm's jaw fell slack. "You fuckin kiddin us?" he said.

Daniel pursed his lips. "That's the crack."

"Jesus Christ, man…" Malcolm sat back, stunned. "I can't fuckin believe that, man. *Fuck*. What an arsehole…What's he thinking, man?"

"What were either of them thinking?"

"Aye, that an'all." Malcolm looked to one side, drummed his fingers on the tabletop. "What're you gonna do?"

"I don't know yet."

"You don't *know*?"

"Oh, I *know* what I'm gonna do, you can fuckin believe that. I don't know *how* I'm gonna do it."

Malcolm took a drink, thought. Stroked his moustache. Absently fingered the bandages on his cut arm where they ended at his wrist. "Whey, John's canny strong. He's dangerous, an'all."

"Aye."

"Got that job comin up, too."

"Aye."

"Bit late to cancel on that now."

"*Aye.*"

Malcolm drummed his fingers a little more. "Why don't you go talk to Steven? See what he has to say. She's still his daughter."

Daniel considered this.

"You're not alone in this, Dan. You've got me.

Anything you need, just say the fuckin word, mate. I'll do it. I mean, the two of us alone, that might not be enough to go after John, but there's others. We just need to put the word out. Some people it's just a case of the price being right, but for the right price anyone'll have yer fuckin back. You're not alone, mate."

Daniel nodded, appreciating Malcolm's words. "All right. Thanks." Daniel got to his feet. "I'm gonna head home."

"Is Mary there?"

Daniel nodded.

Malcolm looked like he was measuring his next words. "How is she?"

"She's not going anywhere."

Malcolm nodded. "All right. Aye."

Daniel went home. Mary was still awake. If she'd tried to get free, he couldn't see any evidence of it.

She looked up at him, frightened. "I'm gonna untie you," he said. "Then I'm gonna go downstairs. If you try to leave…"

Mary nodded that she understood.

Daniel loosened her ankles first, then did her wrists. Mary sat up, rubbed the circulation back into her arms. Daniel struck her across the face with the back of his hand. She stayed down on the mattress, didn't dare to get back up. He could see he'd drawn blood on her cheek. Likely from his wedding ring.

She started to push herself up finally, took her time about it. He wanted to hit her again. His arms shook. He restrained himself. "You stupid fucking cunt." With those words he left her, went back downstairs to make his bed upon the sofa.

He didn't sleep.

Chapter Sixteen

Daniel left Malcolm at the house to keep an eye on Mary. "Constant, mind," he said before he left. "Divvint take yer eye off her for a fuckin second. I divvint care if she needs to piss, you follow her in. Understand?"

"Got it, mate," Malcolm said. "I'll have me beady eye on her the whole while yer out, divvint worry none."

Daniel went to see Steven. Denise wasn't there. "You said this was a private matter," Steven said, letting him into the house. "I sent her out. Is it that kind of private?"

"Aye, probably."

Steven led him through to the sitting room. "Take a seat, lad." Steven lowered himself into his chair, sighing as he did so. "Howay, then. What's the crack?"

Daniel gritted his teeth.

Steven narrowed his eyes, cocked his head. "Somethin wrong with Mary?"

"Kind of, aye." Daniel took a deep breath.

"Just spit it out man, son, will ye?"

"She's been fucking John."

Steven pulled a face like he wasn't sure he'd heard right. "Eh?"

"John. She's been fucking him behind me back. I don't know how long it's been goin on for."

"John? John *Riddell*?"

"Aye."

"What the hell?" Steven pondered this news, rubbed his chin. "Are you sure?"

"Aye, she admitted it."

Steven looked at him. "What'd it take to get her to admit it? Her conscience just get the better of her, she had to come clean, did she?"

"I did what I had to. If she'd grown a fuckin conscience and come to tell me, then maybe I would've gone easy on her. As it happens, I still went pretty fuckin easy on her."

"Whey, you've gotta do what you've gotta do to keep your woman in check sometimes. Even Denise has had to feel the hairy side on a couple of occasions." He raised his hand to fully illustrate his meaning. "But look at her now. No problems with her. Top wife for the Top Man." He grinned. "How's she now? Mary, I mean."

"She's fine. Malcolm's keeping an eye on her."

"Scared she's gonna try and run off?"

"I wouldn't put it past her. Not at the minute."

"All right, then. What d'you wanna do about this nonsense?"

"I wanna kill him."

"Fair enough. That's what I'd wanna do, an'all."

"So you'll sign off on it."

"Aye, but not right now. After the job."

Daniel took a sharp intake of breath. He'd expected this, but it was still no easier to hear. "After?"

"Aye. I want him on the job. It's the day after tomorrow, man, for Christ's sake."

"You expect me to wait until after the job? To fuckin work with him?"

"Aye, I do. And then we all get to take his cut. We might as well get some use out of the cunt before we get rid of him, eh?"

Daniel didn't like it, but clearly Steven had made up his mind. "All right. Fine."

"Who's gonna do it?"

"Me and Malcolm. We might get another guy, just in case."

"Anyone in mind?"

"Jock's gonna be here. He's Malcolm's mate. Malcolm reckons he won't take much talking into it, so long as we pay him right."

"Aye. Can you keep a leash on Mary til then?"

"Yes."

"Good. *After* the job, Daniel."

"I heard you."

"I invited John round here tomorrow, get him acquainted with Jock. You and Malcolm are coming an'all."

Daniel clenched his jaw.

"Keep it together when you're round him, you understand? Don't make him suspicious."

"I'm not worried about that. He already knows I divvint like him."

"Aye, well, divvint let anything slip. You spoke to Jock yet?"

"Not yet."

"Good. Save *that* til after the job, too."

"Aye."

"And after this is all over, you'll wanna do something about keeping a closer eye on that wife of yours. She's always been a runaround, ever since she was a bairn. Hard to keep her under control."

Daniel closed his fists. "You don't need to tell me."

"Stick a bairn in her. Another one. That'll calm her down. She goes the full nine months this time and she'll be far too busy with it to think about running round with other men. I mean, Christ's sake—*John*? You not been cutting it in the bedroom lately, lad?"

Daniel said nothing.

"I didn't even know the two of them knew each other. I've never seen them talking."

"She said they met at your birthday party. I don't know how true that is."

"Really? I suppose I was preoccupied that night. Didn't see much of anything. Don't remember much of what I did see, either."

Daniel had never seen them talk. Whenever he'd looked over, Mary had been alone. Sipping from her glass of wine. Maybe she was lying about that being the night they'd met, but the way he'd been wrenching on her arm, he doubted it. It wasn't like he'd kept a close eye on her the whole time. He'd gone there with the intention of distracting himself with his friends, of getting pissed out of his mind, to forget all about the miscarriage and the wife he was slowly coming to despise but couldn't divorce because of who her father was.

Her father. The fat man sat before him, telling him to put another baby in her.

That would never happen. He'd never touch that whore again. The thought of her made him feel ill.

Daniel looked Steven over. He wasn't the picture of health. One day he'd die. Keel over from either a heart attack or a stroke. Sooner rather than later. That would be the end of the Top Man, and the new one would be ready to step up and take his place.

Him. He would be ready. And once Steven was out the way, he could do whatever he wanted with Mary. Boot her out of his life, never have to look at her miserable face again.

"All right, then." Steven clapped his hands together. "That's sorted. Anything else you wanted to discuss?"

"Nah." Daniel shook his head. "Nah, that's everything for now."

Chapter Seventeen

The job had happened. John had been a part of it. Mary felt like that was significant. Felt like if Daniel was going to do anything, it would be after the job. The thought gave her nervous butterflies. Like anything could happen.

Daniel had gone off somewhere with the big Scottish bloke. Jock, she'd heard them call him. He didn't say much, but he was terrifying. His eyes burned with hatred for everything he looked upon. When he looked at her, Mary felt as if he was imagining all the ways he could hurt her, or worse. A shiver had run through her body. Her blood had run cold.

Wherever they'd gone, Malcolm was still behind. He was always at the house. Always watching her. His arm was still bandaged. He picked idly at a frayed end, looked bored.

Mary sat opposite. Neither of them spoke. They didn't even put the television on. She chewed her lip. Built herself up to ask, "When's it gonna happen?"

Malcolm looked at her. "What?"

"Whatever you're going to do to John. When's it going to happen?"

Malcolm shrugged. "Dunno what you mean, pet." He was a terrible liar.

"Is it tonight? Is that where they've gone?"

He tapped the side of his nose. "You don't need to know when *that's* going to happen. You're better off not knowing."

"Aren't I? Once it's over I might be allowed to leave the house again. I won't need you babysitting us all the bloody time."

"Ah, that'll be lovely, won't it." Malcolm winked at her.

The phone rang. Mary looked at Malcolm. He raised his eyebrows. "Are you gonna answer that?"

"Should I?"

"Whey, would ye normally?"

She hesitated.

"Howay, pet. We can probably both guess who it is. Let's get it over with, eh?"

"What should I say?"

"Nowt. Divvint give anything away. I'm watching ye, mind. Don't do anything to piss us off. I'm gonna be listening carefully."

Mary went closer to the phone, didn't pick it up yet. "He'll want to see me."

"Obviously you can't."

"What should I say?"

"I'm sure you'll think of something."

Mary took a deep breath. She answered the phone. It was John.

They talked longer than she intended. When she asked him if he loved her, Malcolm raised an eyebrow. She didn't care. She wanted to know. Needed to know where she stood, with anyone. If there was anyone that cared about her.

The call ended and she was grateful to put the receiver down. The conversation would have been awkward enough without Malcolm's eyes upon her. The sound of John's voice had made her cold. The voice of a walking dead man.

"So," she said, turning to Malcolm. "Not tonight, then."

"Ye never know, they might be on their way there now."

"I doubt it."

Malcolm shrugged. "Think what you want. Like I said, it's better you don't know. Can't chew you up inside that way."

A thought occurred to her. "You don't know where he lives, do you?"

"We'll find out. He can't stay hidden forever. Who knew the reason he was so secretive about his home was so he could go round shagging other men's wives? You think you were the only one he ever had in there, pet?"

"I don't think about it. It doesn't matter."

"Aye, well. Anyway, that conversation went a bit longer than it needed to, didn't it?"

"Not my fault. I tried to keep it short. You could hear that. He wouldn't take no for an answer."

"John's never struck me as a bloke who takes well to not getting what he wants. Here, anyway, what was the crack with all that?"

"All what?"

"That line of questioning. *Do you love me*. All that shite."

"Curiosity."

"Oh aye. And?"

Mary sat down. "Fuck the bastard."

Malcolm laughed. "You already did, pet. That's why I'm spending night after night with you, instead of me own lass."

"She'll start to get jealous."

"Wor Tina's not the jealous type."

"I wonder how that feels."

"It's fuckin bliss."

"Let me ask you something, Malcolm."

"Aye, sure, whatever. Spit it out."

"How many other women has Daniel slept with?"

"Who says he has?"

"I'm not an idiot, Malcolm. He's obviously getting it from somewhere. He's not getting it from me."

"I wouldn't know anything about that."

Mary shook her head, laughed. "You're so full of shit, Malc."

"Suppose that makes two of us then, eh?"

Mary leaned back on the sofa, got herself comfortable. She wondered how long it would be until Daniel and his new friend got back. "Aye," she said. "Suppose it does."

Chapter Eighteen

Daniel and Jock had dropped the money off with Steven. Steven took Daniel to one side. "How'd it go?"

"Fine. No problems."

"Good. What about the other thing?"

"It'll be soon."

"You asked the big lad yet?" He tilted his head towards Jock.

Jock was in the next room, waiting to leave. "About to."

"Jock can handle himself. He can do all the heavy lifting for ye."

"I've watched him handle himself. He can do the heavy lifting, but he's not gonna be the one that kills the bastard. That's for me."

"Reckon he'll say yes?"

"Malcolm thinks so. Malcolm talks highly of him."

"Aye, him and Malcolm are mates. Even if he turns you down on this, it's not like he'll run off to warn John."

Daniel nodded.

"So, when's it happening?"

"Few days, I reckon."

"Few days? Why you gonna wait so long?"

"Haven't had any time to plan it, man. Had to wait and make sure this job went off all right, didn't I? And if the big lad in there isn't interested, I'm gonna have to gan find someone else."

"Gotta get yer nerve up an'all."

Daniel blinked.

"Never killed anyone before, have ye?"

"Doesn't matter," Daniel said, defensive. "I can do it. Fuckin easy."

Steven shook his head. "It's not easy, son. Not the first time."

"He's been fucking me wife." Daniel leaned closer, showed his teeth. "I can do it. There's no worries in that regard, believe me."

"All right then, son, all right." Steven raised his hands to calm him, but it was clear from his expression that he didn't believe what Daniel said. "Gan have a word with Jock, then. See what he reckons."

Daniel and Jock drove away from Steven's house. Jock didn't say much. Seemed content to sit in silence.

"I wanna talk to you about something," Daniel said.

Jock grunted to show he was listening.

"John, the fella we did the job with, he's been fucking me wife."

Jock turned to look at him. Daniel pulled to a kerb so they could talk properly. He turned in his seat.

"I'm gonna kill him," he said.

Jock nodded agreement. "So ye should."

"John's a tough lad, though. If I'm going after him, I can't miss. And I'm only gonna get the one shot."

"You want some backup?"

"You read me mind. Interested?"

"I could be. So long as the price is right."

"Whey, once he's out the way we'll be getting his share of the cut from today, an'all."

"But I'd want somethin else on top of that. I dinnae come down to Newcastle for the sights. I dinnae gie a toss about yer bridges. I came here to get paid. You want a man dead, that's gonna cost ye extra."

"All right. Name it."

"Three grand."

Daniel whistled through his teeth.

"Things get hairy, you're gonna want to have me around," Jock said. "Trust me. I'm worth every penny. Malcolm can vouch for that."

"I'm sure he can. He already has, more than once."

"Then yes or no."

Daniel nodded. "Aye. Three grand."

"Good. Say the word, tell me the place, I'll be there."

Daniel smiled. He turned to the front. Frost was settling upon the road. Cold was seeping in through their closed windows. He pulled away from the kerb, resumed the journey. The smile remained on his face. Couldn't help himself.

Soon, John would be dead.

And he'd be the one to kill him.

Chapter Nineteen

Daniel was going to make Mary call John to arrange a meet-up. First, Mary got dressed up at his insistence. "Do whatever you'd normally do," he told her. He stayed in the bedroom while she changed her dress, did her make-up.

"If you tip him off, we'll hurt you too," he said, watching her. "If you do it the right way, things don't need to be hard for you. There's a future beyond tonight, ye understand that, don't ye?"

She nodded, putting in earrings.

"You and I, we're still gonna have to live with each other. Things can be tolerable, if you're willing to behave yourself."

"I'm not going to tell him anything."

"Of course not. Now that you know he doesn't love ye."

She paused, looked at him. "Malcolm told ye about that, did he?"

"Tells me everything. Tells me how many times you scratch your nose or fix your hair. Naturally he's gonna tell me every little detail of a phone call." He shook his head. "You fucking idiot. Did you really think he might've loved ye?"

"I don't know what I thought. I suppose that's why I asked."

"Well." Daniel stood. "Now no one fuckin loves ye, do they? You ready yet?"

She ignored his remark. "Aye." She stood too.

"Good. Make the call." He'd plugged the phone in their bedroom back in. He watched her while she dialled the number, arranged the meet. Despite her doing it at his say so, knowing who she was talking to made his blood boil. He bit his tongue until it was over and she put the phone down.

"Let's get a move on, then." They went to leave the room together. Daniel paused, took her wrist. "By the way, feel free to enjoy yerself tonight, pet. It's the last time anyone'll ever fuckin touch ye."

Malcolm and Jock waited downstairs. "We ready to go?" Malcolm said.

Jock stood with his arms folded, face lowered. Looked as mean as ever.

"I dunno," Daniel said. "Are we ready to go, Mary? We don't wanna turn up too early, make him suspicious."

"Let's give it five," Mary said.

"Snow's comin down, mind," Malcolm said. "Divvint wanna give it too long or it'll be too thick to drive through."

Mary took a seat for the wait. Malcolm sat

opposite her, her constant guardian. Jock caught Daniel's eye, tilted his head to one side, to indicate he wanted a word. They left the room together. Daniel closed the door. "What's up?"

"You're sending your wife for John to get on top of again," he said.

"What's the question?"

"Suppose I've got a couple about your thought process."

"Feel free to share them."

"Well, why?"

"Why not? Let John empty his balls before he's dead, and let her fuck her lover-boy one last time. You think I'm ever gonna touch that slut again? After tonight, she's a fuckin celibate spinster. She's me wife in name only."

"And what if she tells him while she's in there with him? What's she got to lose?"

"I don't care if she fucking tells him. What're they gonna do? Try and sneak out together, get away? Ride off into the sunset, live happily ever after? We'll see them. If they leave together, we kill them both."

"Both?"

"Aye. And I'll deal with Steven after, if it comes to that."

"I don't know Steven that well, but I dinnae reckon he'll take well to his only daughter being dead."

"I said I'll deal with it. If I have to. She walks out that building with him, thinking she's running off with him, that's the last straw. That's fucking it."

Jock grinned. "That's what you want her to do, isn't it? That's why you're sending her in at all. Hoping she'll fall in love with him all over again and try to make a break for it."

Daniel checked the time. "Howay, then. Let's go."

Jock wasn't done. He put a hand on Daniel's arm. He didn't squeeze, it wasn't threatening, but the intent was clear. Jock wanted his next words to be taken seriously. "You've got your heart set on John, and that's fine. But if she *does* try to leave with him and you lose yer nerve, just give me the nod."

Daniel bit his lip. "Let's get a move on."

They went out to the car. Malcolm drove. Mary gave directions. Jock and Daniel sat in the back. Daniel didn't know where John lived. Didn't think anyone other than Mary did. He'd always been a secretive bastard.

They parked round the corner. There was a payphone. Mary said there would be. Malcolm stayed in the car. Daniel and Jock got out, followed Mary at a distance, held back as she approached the block of flats. Stayed round the corner so they weren't seen. She got inside and they waited a few minutes. They went to the side of the building, took up position. It was cold. Daniel pulled up his coat collar, stamped his feet. The knife was in his pocket. He wasn't sure what he was going to do with it yet—stab or slice. Stab him right through the fucking heart, or slice his throat and leave him to choke on his own blood. He'd know when the time came. He hoped.

Jock stood still, unaffected by the cold. His hands were in his pockets, that was his only concession. "How long should they be?"

"I don't know," Daniel said.

"Let's hope it's no too long, eh? Dinnae want you standing out here getting embarrassed."

Daniel shot him a look but was too cold to maintain the glare. He kicked snow from his shoes, starting to worry that maybe his hands would be too numb to be of any use. He opened and closed his fists in his pockets, kept the blood flowing.

It was longer than Daniel would have liked. Long enough he started to become suspicious that Mary was trying to warn John. That she really was stupid enough to think they could run away together. Start over.

Daniel could feel his nose begin to run. He turned away from Jock to wipe it. Snorted and spat. Didn't want the big Scot to see him with his nose running. Looking weak.

"There's your missus," Jock said.

Daniel turned. Mary had left the building, was crossing the road. Headed round the corner to where Malcolm was parked. She was alone.

Jock rolled his neck, his shoulders. Popped his joints, loosened up. Daniel remembered he did the same thing before the job. They waited for Mary to reach the car, for Malcolm to make the phone call. For John to leave the building.

Daniel wrapped his hand around the knife.

Squeezed it. Bit his lip. His breath had quickened. He hoped Jock didn't notice. If he had, hopefully he just thought it was the cold. Jock didn't look at him, anyway. Didn't worry about his nerves. He was focused on the front of the building.

Knowing Mary had already left, this was the hardest part. The wait for what came next. The attack. The kill.

Jock slapped Daniel's arm with the back of his hand. He nodded at the building's open front door. "There he is."

Chapter Twenty

Malcolm drove. He'd pulled away from the kerb as soon as he'd got off the phone. Daniel and Jock would make their own way back, after they'd done what they'd gone to do.

Mary felt like she was underwater. Like she was holding her breath. Her eyes were burning. "I don't want to go home," she said.

"Sorry, pet," Malcolm said. "Daniel said to take ye straight there."

"Then drop us off at me parents' house."

Malcolm considered this. "All right." He turned off, took her to them. He drove slowly through the snow.

Mary sat in the back. She chewed on a thumbnail, stared out the window without really seeing anything. She had no idea where she was. Lost in her thoughts. Not paying attention.

Malcolm pulled to a stop. He turned when Mary didn't get out and didn't say anything. "We're here."

She looked up, looked out. Nodded. Pulled on the

door handle.

"I'll wait right here to take ye back," Malcolm said. "Take as long as ye need, like. I've got nowhere else to be."

"Don't wait for me," she said. "I'll make me own way home."

"I divvint think I can do that, mind. Don't think Daniel would be too pleased if I left you alone."

"I'm not going to be alone. And what does it matter? Daniel's got what he wanted now."

Malcolm still appeared unsure.

"I'm with me parents, Malc. And they're probably on his side, anyway. What am I gonna do? I've got nowhere else to go."

"All right, fine. Off ye gan. I'm gonna watch ye til yer inside, mind, so divvint try anything stupid."

Mary didn't bother to respond. What else could she do? Where could she run to? There was nowhere. There was the home with Daniel where she wasn't welcome, and her parents' house. She had nothing else. She got out the car, went up the path to the front door. She could hear the engine idling behind her. She knocked twice but didn't wait for an answer. Pushed the door open and stepped inside.

Her mother approached, took her in her arms. Mary started to cry. She hadn't intended to, but the tears came regardless.

"I know, pet, I know," Denise said, holding her tight and stroking her hair. "You've done something daft, but it's over now. Ye'll never do it again."

Her father appeared in the sitting room doorway. "That done then, is it?"

Mary cried harder. She buried her face into her mother's shoulder so she wouldn't have to answer.

Steven stuffed his hands in his pockets, looked awkward. He shuffled from foot to foot.

"Howay, pet," Denise said, creating some separation. "Let's get you a seat then I'll make ye a nice cup of tea."

Denise took Mary by the arm, led her through to the sitting room, lowered her onto the sofa like she was a small child. Mary allowed herself to be handled. She didn't have any strength. Denise left her, went through to the kitchen. Mary heard her switch the kettle on, the clink as she prepared the cup for the hot water.

Mary wrapped her arms around herself. She was aware of her father watching her, and she tried not to cry. Couldn't show him how she really felt. The knowledge that her life was over. She had nothing anymore. No one. And now she was complicit in a man's death.

A man who didn't love her.

She kept telling herself that. *He didn't love you. He practically said as much. He was just fucking you. Just taking what he could get from you. Same as everyone else. He didn't love you.*

She wondered how things would be if she hadn't had the miscarriage. If the baby hadn't died, if she'd carried it to term and it was here, now, in her empty arms. She could coo at it, kiss its button nose, feed it from her breast and feel satisfied. And Daniel would be satisfied. He'd love her still. He'd touch her still, instead of recoiling from her as if she were diseased. She would never have spoken to John, and it would never have cost him his life.

"How ye doin, then?" her father said.

Mary swallowed, worried that her voice might break. She decided not to answer verbally. Shook her head instead.

"This isn't the end of the world, y'kna," he said. "It'll pass. We'll all move on. You too."

Mary nodded along, but she didn't want to hear it. She wasn't interested in her father's homespun wisdom. She could hear the kettle coming to the boil, beginning to whistle. Soon her mother would return. She felt awkward alone with her father. She knew he had permitted John's murder. She knew Daniel would have come to him to make sure it was all right to go ahead.

He drummed his fingers on the arms of his chair. "You see it happen, did ye?"

"No." Her voice didn't break.

"Probably for the best. So you don't know how they did it?"

"I don't want to know." Though she'd seen Daniel pocket the knife.

"You love him, did ye? John, I mean."

"No." She paused, then added, more firmly, "No."

"You don't sound sure."

"What's it matter anymore?"

"Aye, suppose."

Denise came through, holding the mug of tea in both hands. She handed it over. "Careful, mind," she said. "It'll be red hot."

Mary took the mug, held it. She didn't drink. She stared into the liquid, still spinning where her mother had stirred in the milk and sugar. Denise sat down beside her.

"So," she said. "How long do ye reckon you're gonna be here for? I'm not chasing ye out, pet, I'm just asking. Ye can stay as long as you like."

"I don't know," Mary said. "Maybe a couple of hours. I don't know. Maybe not even that." She bit her lip, then stopped. Tried to control herself. Earlier, with John, it had almost been easy. Slipped straight into their old pattern. It was as if nothing was about to happen, as if they'd never been discovered. As if she didn't know exactly what was going to happen next. She'd kept it together. Her only near slip had come towards the end, as she was leaving, but she'd recovered quickly and didn't think he'd noticed anything.

She'd had a hand in killing a man, and she'd still been able to have sex with him before sending him to his death.

She bit her lip at the thought, and this time didn't try to stop. Bit hard enough it was like she was trying to draw blood. She'd felt like a different person. Able to block out the entirety of the outside world. The knowledge of the situation.

Denise reached over, patted her thigh, squeezed it. "Daniel will get over it," she said. "He's just working his way through it is all. But now he's got nothing to be angry about, has he? It's all been dealt with. He'll still be annoyed at you for a while, aye, but that'll pass. Divvint ye worry. Things will go back to how they were, just make sure you never do anything like that again."

"He won't forget," she said.

"Course he'll never forget," Steven said. "That's to be expected."

Denise waved her husband to be quiet. "He won't forget, but he'll get over it. You can go back to being husband and wife. Maybe try for another bairn, eh? Finally give us a grandchild?"

Mary looked at her mother, and she looked so hopeful. Mary couldn't understand it. All hope was gone. All that remained was darkness.

"Well, yous can both just think about that," Denise said. "In time. It'll come. Trust me."

Mary glanced at her father. He didn't look so sure. Was perhaps a touch more realistic about the situation than her mother was. "Well, it is what it is and it's done now," he said. "Here, Denise, ye not make me a brew, like?"

"I'll make you one after," Denise said, agitated.

"Ye've just had the kettle on, like, is all I'm sayin."

"Just hold yer horses, Steve. Yer daughter's upset, man. I'll make ye a cup of tea in a minute."

"Here, Dad, have this one," Mary said, offering

her cup.

"No, I made that for you," Denise said, forcing the cup back to where it had been resting in her lap, held by both hands.

"I don't think I can drink it."

"Make yourself," Denise said. "It'll help you feel better."

"Listen, Mary," Steven said. She looked up. "It's no good moping, is it? How many times can I say the same thing—it's done. You've made yer bed, now you're gonna have to lie in it."

Mary knew that. Didn't need her father to tell her. She drank the tea. It had cooled. She drank it all down. "Aye, okay," she said, looking down into the bottom of the cup, the stray tea leaves there and the molecules of sugar that hadn't dissolved. "I'm gonna get away now," she said.

"Are ye sure, pet?" Denise said.

"Aye." She got to her feet. "I've gotta get back some time, haven't I?"

"Ye want us to call ye a taxi?" Steven said.

"Or we could give you a lift," Denise said.

It was clear from the look on Steven's face that he didn't want to give her a lift anywhere. Didn't want to leave the warm house. He was comfortable in his chair and unwilling to be moved from it.

"No, I want to walk," Mary said. She forced a smile. "It'll do me good."

Her mother took her to the door, hugged her before she left, but her father stayed where he was. He called through as the door opened—"Bye, Mary."—but wasn't there to see her off. Denise stayed at the door, watched her go until she was out of sight.

Mary took her time walking. It was cold, but she didn't register it. Her shoes crunched through the snow and she was careful not to slip. The occasional snowflake landed on her cheek, ran like a tear as it melted, but she didn't cry anymore. All her tears were gone.

She didn't keep track of the time, but it had been dark for a while when she finally got home. Daniel was there, waiting for her. He was in the sitting room, a drink in hand. "Your boyfriend's dead," he said. He swirled the liquid in its glass. It looked like whisky. He took a drink, swirled it some more, stared into it. He looked up at her, his lip curled like the sight of her was akin to a bad smell. "Where've you been?"

"I was at my parents'. Malcolm didn't tell you?"

"He told me. You've been a while."

"I walked back."

"Mm." He grunted. "Aye, I can feel the cold coming off you. You look blue, mind."

She shrugged. She still couldn't feel it.

"Thought you'd probably stay over."

"No," she said. "I just didn't want to come straight back here."

Daniel shrugged then. "Please yerself. I'd rather ye didn't come back at all, but here ye are."

They stayed in silence for a while, Daniel sitting

and drinking, Mary standing with snow melting and dripping from her. Eventually she took off her coat, as if she'd decided she would stay, and hung it up. She slipped out of her shoes.

"I'll be getting a bed for the spare room," Daniel said. "That'll be my room from now on. Don't disturb me when I'm in there. As far as you're concerned, that part of the house no longer exists. You got that?"

"Yes."

"We're husband and wife in name only. Frankly, I just want you to keep out of my way. You don't ever again address me like we're a couple—don't even talk to me like we're friends. I don't expect anything from you other than to look after the house. Keep it tidy, that's all. You don't need to cook for me, I'll take care of myself in that regard. Just keep the house clean. And let me make something crystal clear—never bring a man in here. Ye got that? You bring a man in here, I'll kill *him* an'all."

"Are you going to bring women in here?" Mary said. She kept her face lowered.

Daniel's eyes narrowed. He drained the drink then stood. He squeezed the glass. Didn't say anything for a while, just stared at her. Then he turned suddenly, threw the glass at the wall. It shattered, glass sprayed. Mary flinched. Daniel turned back to her. "I don't reckon that's any of your business. Just stay out of my way, all right, Mary? Just stay *right* out of my way, and we'll get along just fine."

He left the sitting room, headed for the stairs. He

paused before he reached them. "Ye can make a start on keeping the house tidy by clearing up that glass," he said. "I'll have the bed tonight, you can have the settee." He stared at her. Mary looked back. She wasn't trying to be defiant. She was too tired for that. She was defeated. "Get out of my sight," he said, practically spitting the words. "I can't fuckin look at you."

He didn't wait for her to do as he said and get out of his sight. Instead, he turned, went up the stairs. Mary was left alone in the sitting room. She took a step forward and collapsed into a chair. The broken glass was scattered across the ground next to the fireplace. She stared at it. Stared at it until her eyes began to close, and she fell asleep.

Part Three
Wooler, Newcastle, Hamilton
1978 to 1979

Chapter Twenty-One

The wound across his neck was an ugly scar. Stray strands of stubble poked through the mangled, puckered flesh where he couldn't get at them with a razor.

John washed away the leftover soap, studied the scar. He'd been bearded before the shave, leaving the hair on his face and neck to grow as the wound had healed. His hair had gotten longer than he'd have liked, too. He'd hacked it off. He was no hairdresser, but it was presentable.

John left the tiny bathroom, passed through the cabin into the bedroom, pulled on his clothes. A pair of jeans, a tatty old T-shirt, a thick jumper to protect him against the cold. The cabin was his. Hidden away in woodland on the outskirts of Wooler. A hideout for after hot jobs, or when he found himself in hot water.

The water was the hottest it had ever been.

He went outside, gathered chopped wood, carried it back in and stoked a fire. It didn't take much to warm the cabin, but once the fire was dead, it would become freezing. The wind and the chill found its way inside through every available gap.

The snow had melted. It had been a few months since he'd been left to die in it, lying on the frozen ground with his hot blood running out of him. It wasn't quite spring yet, but it was warmer than when he'd first got to the cabin.

He was biding his time. Healing. John could be patient when he had to be. Now was one of those times. His neck being slit from ear to ear necessitated his patience.

But it wouldn't last. Already he was plotting his return to Newcastle. That's what kept him going. That's what had forced him to get up when he'd been left for dead.

Revenge.

He took a seat near the fire, warmed his hands. It was a scar now. Healed. It wouldn't be long. Some push-ups, some pull-ups, a couple of runs, and he'd be fighting fit. He'd be going back for them, for all of them, and for the money they didn't give him. The money owed, and then some.

No doubt they knew he was still alive. Or, at the very least, that his body had gone missing. Maybe they'd assumed he'd tried to crawl for assistance, had died elsewhere. A bin, maybe, seeking warmth and protection from the snow. Taken away with the rest of the rubbish when the bin man made his rounds.

He was sure they weren't that stupid. John was a survivor, and they knew that. They'd have kicked themselves, hard, at the realisation his body wasn't where it should have been. Told themselves they should have stayed behind, made sure it was done. Stick the knife in him again. Through the eye this time, or the heart.

That was Daniel's mistake. He didn't have a clue what he was supposed to be doing. Never killed a man, clearly. Too quick to walk away. Jock surprised him, though. He'd had him pegged as a professional. Perhaps it had been his first time too, though John doubted that. He'd had no vested interest in John's death, other than what they were undoubtedly paying him to help, and likely just phoned his assistance in. Still, John was surprised. Not least of all because *now* he had a vested interest, even if he didn't know it.

Jock was on the list.

Jock was going to die.

John watched the flames. Thought about that knife slicing through his skin. His blood spilling. He saw Daniel's face in the fire. "Not deep enough, ye stupid twat." His voice had become scratchy and gruff, from both the attack and lack of use. There was no one to talk to up here. No one nearby. No one knew where he was. It would stay that way. This cabin was his and his alone. He'd never told anyone about it.

The fire crackled and popped. Wood burnt to ash collapsed in on itself. John stared at it, thought about his fury, about his revenge. About what had happened to him. How it would not stand.

Thought about his list.
Daniel.
Jock.
Malcolm.
Steven.
Mary.

Chapter Twenty-Two

It could have been the cold of the snow under his cheek that kept him awake. Kept his eyes wide as he watched the blood pumping out, the red soaking into the white and spreading further and further outward.

Or it could have been his indignation that someone had attempted to kill him.

Whichever it was, there were two options available to him. No more than that, only two. It was always the same. Any life-or-death situation. Any fight he'd ever been in where he'd gotten knocked down. He could stay where he was and die, or he could get up and move.

He chose the second option. He always did.

He was weak, getting weaker, but he found strength enough to force his arms under himself, to raise his hands to his neck, to grab the wound by the flaps that had been cut into it and try his best to force them closed. They were slick, hard to get a grip on. He grabbed snow, rubbed it across the cut, soaked up the blood, tried again with numb and shaking fingers. All ten of them, squeezing.

With his elbows he pushed himself from the ground. Dragged up his legs to get his knees under himself.

He was upright. Now he needed to stand.

He leaned to the side so his shoulder was pressed to the wall, used it for support. His feet nearly slipped out from under him as he straightened, but he managed to keep his balance. If he fell, he might not get back up. The blood was running through his fingers still, but it wasn't spraying. John noted this. A good sign. Probably enough had been cut to kill him, but nothing serious that could kill him fast. He started walking. One foot in front of the other. Remaining vigilant, wary, looking round in case Daniel and Jock were still nearby. They wouldn't react well to him being on his feet.

Move. He told himself to walk. Not to look back. Not to think too much, to concentrate only on the task in hand, which was to keep himself alive. There'd be time to think later. *Just keep moving.*

The streets were empty, people sheltering inside, away from the snow. John walked for ten minutes, maintaining the death grip on his neck, before he spotted a taxi. It was parked at the kerb, the engine still running. He could see the driver inside, drinking a steaming cup of tea or coffee from a flask and reading a newspaper. He wore a flat cap low over his eyes, and a thick coat and scarf. John went to him, his legs almost giving out beneath him.

Just keep moving.

He opened the door and got inside. The driver gave a start, almost tore his newspaper. Then he turned, saw the mess his new passenger was in, spilled his tea. "Jesus Christ!" He turned, like he was going to try and escape his own car. John used the last of his strength to grab him by the back of his shirt. Whatever little remained, it was enough. The driver couldn't get out, made a choked sound as his collar hit his throat. He turned back, eyes wide, all colour gone from his cheeks.

John tried to talk but couldn't. He grunted, growled, gesticulated. The driver nodded, eyes still wide. "Okay, okay," he said, eager to please, terrified the crazed man was going to try and hurt him. He looked out the car, checked the streets to make sure his new fare hadn't been pursued, that whoever had attacked him wasn't coming to finish him off and, in the process, his new driver, too.

The taxi started rolling, taking its time through the snow. John leaned forward, pointed where he wanted him to go. John could feel his eyes trying to close. He battled against them. Slapped himself. They reached Gosforth. He pointed down a street, grunted and tugged on the driver's collar to make him pull over. John got out the car, stumbled to Dr Mitchell's front door. The driver didn't hassle him for payment. He drove off.

John knocked, looked back down the pathway. Drops of blood had marked his journey. Snow was still coming down. Hopefully the fresh fall would cover the red dots, cover any trace of his arrival.

The door opened. It was Doug. He pulled an impromptu impression of the taxi driver as he looked upon John. Same wide eyes, same slack mouth. If he'd been holding anything to drop, he would've dropped it.

John tried to take a step forward. All strength had left him. His indignation had brought him here, to Gosforth, to the doctor. To the one man that could possibly save his life, if he didn't instantly hand him straight over to Steven and Daniel.

John's eyes were closing. He couldn't battle them anymore. He fell forward, into Doug's arms, and hoped for the best.

Chapter Twenty-Three

John drove down to Newcastle.

It felt good to be out the cabin, to be on the road. Returning. It felt good to know what was coming next.

The weather had changed since he'd seen the city last. The snow was gone, but it was no less grim. Grimmer, in fact. Grey clouds hung low, spat rain at the ground. It was the middle of the day but there weren't many people on the street, and those that were hurried along with umbrellas, or coats pulled up to protect themselves as best they could. Most of those he saw carried shopping bags, seemingly unable to wait for the weather to pass.

John went by Malcolm's block of flats first. He parked opposite, sat there for an hour. He didn't expect to see anything, didn't expect to see Malcolm or Tina. He was touching base. Taking in the city. Marking his targets. If he did happen to spot them, good. He'd see them. Freshen his rage, though it still burned deep within, despite his outwardly calm appearance.

The block stood solemn and grey, darkened by the downpour. All the while he sat there, he saw only one person enter the building. A little old lady. She was nothing to him. He moved on. Went by the Top Man's house.

The view of its front was mostly concealed by the hedges that lined its wall. He parked over the road. He didn't stay there as long. He'd be easier to spot on a street, in front of a house, than in front of a block of flats.

Again, there wasn't much to see. He popped his knuckles, watched the upstairs windows. He saw movement at one of them. It looked like Denise. Bending over, gathering up washing. Her husband's dirty clothes. The woman spent her life cleaning up after her fat, lazy husband. Cooking for him, cleaning for him. She probably spoon-fed him and wiped his arse.

John moved on.

He thought about Jock as he drove. He didn't know where he was, where he could be. Doubted he'd still be in Newcastle. Likely he'd returned to Scotland. John wasn't concerned. He had a plan for finding Jock.

He made his way to Daniel's house.

Saved the worst for last.

Thoughts of wrapping his hands around Daniel's throat had kept him going. They'd warmed him on cold nights.

Except that wouldn't be enough.

There'd been so many more thoughts. All the ways he could torture him. He wanted to make it slow. Wanted to make him scream, cry, beg for mercy.

Mercy that would be a long time coming.

It wouldn't be hard. John knew Daniel would cry. He was soft. He put on a hard front, but that's all it was. He was nothing. A scared little boy running round with the big lads, acting tough for their benefit. He was in over his head.

John reached the house. Daniel and Mary. He wondered if they were still together. If their marriage had survived the discovery of what Mary had been up to.

Sometimes he'd wondered how the truth had come out. Had Mary come clean? Had Daniel found out of his own volition?

Why had she had sex with him the last time they'd seen each other, when she'd been setting him up for death? He found it hard to believe she was truly that cold, though the circumstance spoke for itself.

He had a lot of questions, but he didn't care about the answers. The answers were unimportant. What was done was done. Now he was back, and they would all suffer for it.

He stared at the house. As with the others, with the exception of the glimpse of Denise, he saw nothing. No activity at the windows. Too early for lights to be on.

His anger rose. The knowledge that perhaps Daniel was right there, so close. Nothing stopping him from getting out the car, going up to the front door and finding out. Enjoying the look on Daniel's face as he saw who it was and realised what was about to happen.

No.

He had to wait. To anticipate. To know it was coming and yet also know there was nothing he could do about it.

John took a deep breath. Calmed himself. He idly fingered the scar across his neck. The leering grin cut in by Daniel that would now always be a part of him.

John stayed longer than he intended. Just watched. School must have finished somewhere as children began to walk by, hand in hand with their mothers. He started the engine and drove on. He watched the house as it receded in the mirror, like he hoped to catch a glimpse of someone. Daniel or Mary, he wasn't sure who he wanted to see more. His hands wrapped tight around the steering wheel as if Daniel's neck was already between them.

Slow. He'd kill Daniel slow.

Mary...

For Mary, he'd make it fast.

Chapter Twenty-Four

Mary left her bedroom. It was too loud upstairs.

She went down, the rhythmic banging of the headboard against the wall in Daniel's room drilling through her skull. He'd positioned his bed so the headboard pressed against the wall that joined to hers. She was sure he'd done it on purpose.

Mary had been reading in her room—what used to be *their* room—when he got back. She hadn't seen the woman. Assumed it was a new one. It was always a new one. She took a seat in the sitting room, still carrying her book. She tried to read, but the banging persisted. She could hear laughter, too. Grunts, groans, giggles. She thought about putting on a record, but there was nothing she wanted to listen to. She thought about going out, taking a walk, but it was raining hard.

But, more than that, no matter what, this was her *home*. She shouldn't have to leave it. Daniel did it on purpose. To upset her. Torture her. He was trying to drive her out, she was sure of it. She wouldn't leave.

He would break before she did.

She got up, went into the kitchen, put the kettle on. She stared out at the rain, watched as it ran down the glass. The kettle drowned out the sounds from upstairs. By the time it had boiled, the noises had stopped. Upstairs was silent. Mary took her tea through to the sitting room, resumed her book.

An hour passed. Mary began to wonder if this one would be staying the night. That always led to a pleasant morning after. Sometimes she made them breakfast. Nearly always a cup of tea. They were surprised to see her. Didn't know anyone else lived in the house. Didn't know Daniel was married. He always took off his wedding ring when he went out. Left it off most of the time. Only ever put it on when he had to see her father.

So. That's what her life had become. A tea maker for her husband's various mistresses.

It wouldn't stay like this. Mary was going to get out. She wasn't sure how, or when, but she refused to let this be her lot. She would move on, go somewhere else and start over. She wasn't sure where yet. South? North to Northumberland, or further north, to Scotland? Abroad?

In her room, hidden under her bed—not that Daniel ever searched—were brochures for foreign countries. Spain, Majorca, Benidorm. She even had one for America. They were all for package holiday resorts, though if she was going to run, she was going somewhere to stay. They had pictures of the surrounding areas, though. Of the country. She'd flick through their glossy pages late into the night and dream of escape.

Daniel's bedroom door opened upstairs. She heard footsteps coming down, but only one set. It was Daniel. He entered the sitting room. Didn't look at her. He went straight to the phone, dialled a number. He was calling a taxi. After the call, he put the receiver down. He was going to walk away, return upstairs. Maybe squeeze in a quickie before the taxi arrived. Mary wondered if it was just for the woman, or if he'd be leaving with her.

She cleared her throat. Daniel kept walking. "Do you have to be so loud?" she said.

He turned back. His eyes, when they looked upon her, were dead. She may as well have not been there. He looked right through her. "Do you always have to be home?" he said. He didn't wait for a response. Turned and went back upstairs. She heard the door close.

He'd asked if she always had to be home, but he already knew the answer.

Yes.

She did.

Because of him. He wouldn't let her go anywhere else. Didn't trust her to visit friends, knowing that was the excuse she'd been making when she went to see John. She wasn't sure what he thought she could accomplish. She never saw anyone, never spoke to anyone. It was highly unlikely she'd be able to nip out, find a man to seduce, and begin a new affair.

It had occurred to her, long before, that regardless of John, Daniel had already fallen out of love with her. Since the miscarriage that he blamed her for. John was just an excuse to make his dislike more apparent. And what was more, the fact of what had happened with John meant no one blamed him for his attitude. Not even her parents.

They knew what was happening. They wouldn't admit it, not out loud, but they knew. If pressed, they would say she'd brought it on herself.

She'd made her bed.

Outside, a car beeped its horn. The taxi. Upstairs, the bedroom door opened again. Two sets of feet on the stairs now, coming down. Mary saw the girl, finally. She was younger than Mary. Long dark hair, permed. She was laughing about something Daniel had said. She saw Mary on the sofa and her mouth clamped shut, her head cocked to one side, surprised, confused. She started to raise a hand to point, opened her mouth to ask who this woman was, but Daniel cut her off. "Don't mind her," he said. "She just lives here." He ushered her to the door.

He'd told one girl Mary was his sister. He'd told another she was the cleaner.

The front door opened. It promptly closed. He didn't stay on the step to wave her away. He came back through, went to the stairs, stopped. He stepped back into the room. "Why do ye do this?" he said.

Mary blinked. "Do what?"

"This." He indicated her sitting on the sofa.

"Make a spectacle of yerself like this. Sitting out in the open where everyone can see ye."

"Making a spectacle of myself?" Mary wasn't sure what she was hearing. "This is my home, Daniel. I'm just sitting in it. Do ye really wanna talk about making a *spectacle*?"

He sneered.

"I'm just minding me own business, man. Is that not what you wanted? And I came downstairs so I didn't have to hear all that bloody noise the two of you were making. She was a particularly loud squealer, wasn't she?"

Daniel smirked, though Mary hadn't meant it to be humorous and he knew it. "Aye," he said. "She really was. Y'kna what else?"

Mary didn't respond. Whatever it was, she was sure she didn't want to know.

Daniel was undeterred. "She was a far better shag than you ever were." He walked away with that, went back upstairs, to his room.

Mary rolled her eyes. Daniel maybe thought those childish barbs still cut her, but they didn't. She'd heard them too long, and in too many variations. She was numb to them now. She drank her tea, picked up her book, continued her reading. Thought about escape.

The house, at least, was finally silent.

Chapter Twenty-Five

John woke in a strange bed.

He gave a start, sat upright. His hands went straight to his neck. It was bandaged. His head was pounding. His hands shook. His skin was pale. He took a deep breath. It hurt.

Every movement hurt. He grimaced as he swung his legs over the side of the bed, looked round. The walls were cream, a framed expressionist French painting hung on the one opposite. The bed was a single in a spare bedroom. There was nothing else in it. John went to the window, looked out, down onto the street below. He was at the doctor's house. He remembered falling into his arms. The doctor must have caught him. Stitched the wound shut, bandaged him up, carried him to the bed. He wondered how much the doc's family had seen.

John checked the road for cars he might recognise, or people. He saw none. The snow that covered the ground was fresh and thick.

He felt unsteady on his feet and returned to the

bed to sit down, to gather himself. In a pile in the corner he saw a pair of pants, a fresh shirt. He looked down and realised he was still dressed in his bloodied clothes. It had darkened, hardened, it crumbled at his touch. The buttons on his shirt had been torn open, likely by the doctor to get at him.

There was no mirror in the room, but John reckoned he looked like hell. He thought about how bad the wound must look, under the bandage. He rubbed his cheeks, felt the scrape of thick stubble. Wondered how long he'd been there.

He needed to move.

He stripped off his bloodied clothes, put on the fresh ones in the corner. They were loose on his frame. John looked down at his stomach, felt it with his hands. He'd lost weight. Could be it was all the blood he'd spilled.

He balled up the bloodied clothes, held them under his arm, left the room. Paused on the landing. The upstairs was quiet. He could hear movement below. Not much, just a little. Something scraping on a tabletop. From the kitchen, perhaps. John went down to the sound, took his time, holding onto the railing as he went. Everything was spinning, but he persisted. He felt breathless. His heart was pounding already. At the foot of the stairs, in the hallway, there was a mirror. The face looking back shocked him. It was pale, skeletal. The eyes were sunken, the skin below them dark. Again, John questioned how long he'd been at the house.

"Thought I could hear you coming down," Doug said. John turned. He was in the kitchen doorway. "Ye divvint kna when to stay down, do ye?"

"So I'm told," John said. His voice was scratchy, barely above a whisper.

"Howay, come take a seat," Doug said. "Let's have a look at ye."

John shuffled along after him, followed him into the kitchen, to the table where he'd stitched the wound in Malcolm's arm. Where John had maybe had his neck stitched closed, too. He couldn't remember any of it.

John collapsed into the chair. Felt the aches that coursed through his body. He hated being so weak, so helpless.

Doug checked his pupils, put his hand to his forehead to feel his temperature. "How do you feel?"

"Like shit."

"There's no fever. So that's good. Let me get you something to eat. You'll be weak."

John grunted. "How long have I been here?"

"You've been out for three days."

John spun in the chair. He'd moved too fast, he felt dizzy, like he might throw up.

"Slow down, John," Doug said. "Take your time. You need to recover. You shouldn't even be out of bed yet. You lost a lot of blood. I mean, how you even made it here…" Doug shook his head. "You're something else, you are."

John swallowed. It hurt to do so. "Are they

looking for me?"

Doug nodded. "Oh aye, they're looking for you. Came here."

John stared at the doctor. Assumed he hadn't given him up, or else he wouldn't have woken up.

"Don't worry. I didn't tell them anything."

"That oath of yours, eh?"

"Suppose so. But I don't owe anyone anything, either. I wasn't gonna let them come into my house and kill you when my family were right here. My kids."

"What if they hadn't been?"

"Well, then I guess it would've been the oath that kept me from telling them you were here."

John nodded his thanks. "I appreciate it, doc. Where's the family now?"

"They're staying at the wife's mother's house. After Daniel and the lads came round, the missus decided they wanted to be somewhere else."

"Sorry to put you all out like this."

Doug didn't answer that. He turned, busied himself at the counter. John wondered if the doctor and his wife were having relationship difficulties due to the clandestine nature of his extracurricular activities.

"Here." Doug put down a glass of orange juice, a plate of toast. "Eat that and drink that. They'll help. You need something in ye."

John needed to move, to get out of the city, find somewhere safer to rest and recover, but he ate first. The doctor was right. He needed something inside him, to keep him going. He started eating, tried to eat fast but couldn't.

"Slow down, big man," Doug said. "Just take yer time, it's not going anywhere."

Doug thought he rushed because he was hungry. It wasn't that. John was feeling antsy. Now he was fully awake and apprised of the situation, he wanted to get gone. To regroup. To plan.

Doug sat back in his chair, sipped on his tea. John took a drink of the orange juice. His throat hurt. Everything hurt.

"The missus had to give me a hand with you," Doug said. "Don't think she was particularly pleased about that, but I needed the help. We'd just put the bairns to bed an'all. Settled in for a quiet night, next thing we know we've got you spread out on this very table."

"You ever just eat at this thing?"

Doug laughed. "All the time. We always make sure we get rid of the blood."

John folded a piece of toast into a small lump, popped it into his mouth. He tore the rest of the slice into small pieces, repeated. Easier to eat that way. Less chewing, less difficulty swallowing.

Doug saw what he was doing. "Your throat will be swollen," he said. "It'll go down. It'll just take plenty rest and fluids is all." He grinned, shook his head. "You really are somethin else, aren't ye? Turn up here holding yer neck closed. Bloody hell, man. Ye just won't do what you're supposed to, will ye?"

"What am I supposed to do?"

"Whey, when someone cuts yer throat, yer supposed to die."

"Don't have time for that."

Doug laughed. "Who does?"

"They didn't cut deep enough."

"Oh, they cut deep enough. Aye, if they were gonna cut you up and leave you to die they probably should've gone deeper, but believe me there's plenty people out there who would be dead with what happened to you. That's gonna leave a nasty scar. I mean, how they managed to avoid anything serious…You're very lucky."

"Aye. They're not."

Doug held up his hands. "I don't wanna hear anything about that. I just put the lot of ye back together, that's all. Anything that comes next, I don't wanna hear about it."

John nodded, though he'd had no intention of telling him. John looked down at his plate. He was nearly finished. He took another drink. "I'll be going soon."

"Wherever you go, make sure you rest."

"Right. What do you want to do about these clothes I'm wearing?"

"Keep them. It's fine."

"I need a bag for these. I'll take them with me." He indicated the bloodied clothes he'd brought down with him, dumped on the table when he sat.

Doug got up, went to the cupboard under the sink, pulled a bag out from under it, handed it over.

John packed the clothes. He caught his breath. Every exertion was making him breathless. It was frustrating. He finished the toast and the juice. Doug had sat back down. John looked at him.

"Don't breathe a word of this to anyone," he said. "You never saw me."

"I already didn't."

"You might change your mind. The fact that you didn't when you had the chance is the only reason I haven't already killed you."

Doug raised an eyebrow. "Ye think you're in any condition?"

"You think I was in any condition to make my way here three nights ago?"

Doug ground his teeth. "I saved your life. I've already covered for you once. I don't appreciate being threatened."

"Good. This isn't a threat. I'll be gone for a while, but I will be back, Doug. If I find out you've told them anything, I'll come back here." He stared hard. His eyes had lost none of their power. Doug shifted in his chair. He nodded. "Say it."

"I've already said it, man," Doug said. "I'm not gonna tell anyone anything. You think I want the hassle?"

John started to gather himself, to get to his feet. "When I come back, I'll pay you then."

"I'd rather you didn't come back here, John."

"You won't see me. I'll put it through the letter box. I'll stick it in an envelope. It won't be marked, but it'll be from me." John had talked too much. The sound of his voice had lowered more. Was a whisper now. He cleared his throat. It hurt to do so.

"Let me get your shoes," Doug said, standing. "I put them out the way. Figured whoever'd tried to kill ye might come looking, wanted them hidden in case they were recognised."

John followed. Doug went into a shoe cupboard in the hallway near the front door. As he turned his back, bent over, John thought about dumping his clothes out the bag in his hand, wrapping the bag around Doug's head, suffocating him. Dead men can't talk.

But his wife had seen John, too. Helped to stitch him together. If he killed Doug, he'd have to kill her too. He didn't know where she was, didn't have the time to search. If he killed Doug, she'd know it had been him. Once she started talking, word would spread. Killing Doug wasn't worth the hassle. He didn't like to do it, but the best thing was to blindly hope Doug would keep his word and say nothing.

He turned, John's shoes in hand. "Cheers," John said, taking them, moving off to the front door and slipping into them.

Doug watched him. John reached for the door, opened it. "I'd say it's been a pleasure," Doug said. "But I'd be lying."

John winked at him. "That's what everyone says. I'm beginning to think it's maybe me."

He left, closed the door. The cold hit him hard.

The snow was thick on the path before him. He looked up and down the street, made sure it was clear, no one round. John started walking. He turned left, went to the end of the street, turned the corner. Made sure it was still quiet. It was. He found a car, broke into it, hotwired it. Didn't stop to catch his breath until he'd pulled his way. He pointed the car north, out of the city. North, to his cabin.

Chapter Twenty-Six

John had gone back to Malcolm's block of flats. He'd sit there for longer than an hour this time, if needed. He'd sit there all night and into the next morning, if he had to.

He doubted it, though. He was playing a hunch, but Malcolm wasn't the kind to sit in night after night. He and Tina, they both went out a lot. Pubs and clubs. Malcolm liked a drink, even if he couldn't handle it all that well.

John watched the front of the building, waited. It started to get dark. John settled into his chair. He worked himself from side to side a little, loosened up his spine, didn't want to get too stiff in the car.

People came and went. None of them Malcolm or Tina. None of them he recognised.

John waited. Patient. This was the beginning. He was back, and ready to take his revenge. The beginning would take as long as it would take. After that, he knew things would move fast.

It was eight o'clock at night. Malcolm and Tina

left the building. John stayed low. They didn't come to his side of the road. They walked arm-in-arm, talking. Continued on down the road. John let them get some distance, then he got out the car, followed. He stayed on the opposite side of the road, never took his eyes off them.

They reached a pub and went inside. John stayed out. Found a spot in the shadows opposite, leaned against the wall and resumed his wait.

They were inside for an hour, then they moved on. John followed. Still just the two of them. They didn't accumulate any followers, a group. That was good. John wanted it to stay that way.

They went into a club this time. John found another spot to lean and wait. People passed him by. Nobody paid him any mind. Nobody cared. He wouldn't be the only man standing in shadows for no discernible reason in Newcastle that night, or any other night.

John could hear music coming from inside, but it was muffled and he didn't recognise it. His eyes never left the front of the building. There was a bouncer there. He either hadn't seen John or was ignoring him.

A couple of hours passed. It was getting late. The people that passed by on the street were noticeably drunker. Someone stumbled beside him. "Oh, sorry mate, didn't see ye there," he said, flashing a sloppy smile. "Here, have ye got a light?" He held up a cigarette.

John looked past him, at the front still. "Keep moving," he said.

"Eh?"

The man's friend wasn't as drunk. He saw John, sensed the implicit violence that came from him in waves, took his friend by the arm and moved him on.

More time passed. Malcolm and Tina seemed to enjoy this club. They were in no hurry to leave. It was close to midnight.

A couple nearly fell through the front door as they left. Malcolm and Tina were behind them. They saw the couple in front trip, were laughing about it. The unknown couple went one way, Malcolm and Tina went the other, as if they were heading home. John looked up the road. The route before them was clear. He pushed himself from the wall, rolled his shoulders, followed. Popped his knuckles as they walked. Ready to hit something. Someone.

He quickened his pace as they neared an alleyway, bore down on them and tackled them to one side, into it. They swore at him, startled. He hit Tina first. A sharp blast across her jaw that knocked her down. Her head bounced off the ground. He turned on Malcolm, gave him the same treatment, but kept hold of him, stopped him from following her down. Pulled the punch a little. Enough to knock him dizzy. Followed up with a couple of blows to the stomach, knocked the wind out of him. Held him up by the collar and put his face close to his ear. "Let's take a walk."

Malcolm's head rolled on his neck. He saw John. He pissed his pants. John saw it pooling round his shoes. Could smell it.

"Keep calm, and keep yer mouth closed," John said. "Behave yourself and you'll be able to come back and pick yer lass up."

Malcolm's mouth worked. Nothing came out but air.

John put his arm around Malcolm, hauled him from the alleyway. Tina lay on the ground still. She wasn't moving. John didn't bother to check if she was still breathing.

Malcolm was gasping. John thought he was crying, too. He dragged him along the streets. Malcolm kept tripping over his own feet. John kept him upright. "That's a good lad," John told him. "Just keep yer mouth shut for now. Not a fuckin peep. This will all be over soon."

The Tyne Bridge came into view. They went to it. A couple of cars passed by, but no one paid them any attention. Just a drunk being held up by his friend. Aided home.

John took Malcolm to the midpoint of the bridge. They stopped. No one else on it. Malcolm caught his breath. John pressed him into the railing. Malcolm found his voice.

"John, John, mate, I swear to you—"

"I'm not interested, Malcolm. I just want you to answer me questions is all."

"But John, I promise, swear on me mam's life, man, I didn't—"

"I don't wanna hear it, Malcolm. I already told ye. Ye helped them try to kill us, that's all there is to it. I don't wanna hear yer excuses. I know they're lies. You're just embarrassing yerself and insulting me."

Malcolm clamped up.

"That's better. Now, like I told ye, if you behave yerself and play nice, tell me everything I wanna know, you'll be fine. Everything'll be all right. I always liked you, Malcolm. You can walk off this bridge and go back and find Tina. I'm sure she'll wake up with a banging headache. She'll need you there to take care of her."

Malcolm nodded, eager to get this over with. John saw the way his eyes focused on John's neck in the dim light, fixated by the wicked scar.

"Yer mate Daniel's not very good with a knife. Didn't surprise us, to be honest."

Malcolm swallowed, looked up into his eyes. John could see his fear. Could smell it on him, stronger than the piss that soaked the front of his pants.

"I took a drive round the Toon when I got back," John said. "Checked out all the old haunts. Obviously you and Tina were still in the same place. What about everyone else?"

Malcolm had to clear his throat before he could speak again. "No one's moved, if that's what ye mean."

"That's exactly what I mean. All still in the same houses?" John ran off the door numbers and addresses for Steven and Denise, Daniel and Mary.

"Aye, that's right," Malcolm said.

"Good. Glad to hear it. What about Jock?"

"He's not here anymore. He left after…whey, after you. Went back up to Scotland."

John grinned, showed his teeth. "So how do I find him?"

Malcolm gave an address. Gave directions. John memorised them. Recited them back. Malcolm nodded. John could feel his body loosening against his own, thinking it was nearly over.

"Good lad, Malcolm," he said. "I appreciate you playing nice like this, really do. Here's one last question for ye. Did the doctor say anything about me while I was gone?"

"Doug? No, no he didn't. He help you, did he?"

"I'm glad to hear that, Malcolm. For his sake. Anyway, we're done here." He punched Malcolm in the stomach, doubled him over. There were no cars, no people. He couldn't hear an engine anywhere near. He started to lift Malcolm over the railing.

"John, no, *no*! Howay, man! I telt ye everything! No!"

John kept lifting. The top half of Malcolm's body was over, only his legs still on the bridge side of the railing. He faced down into the black water below.

"No, John, no! Please! I can't swim, man!"

John paused. Leaned down a little to be sure Malcolm could hear him. "Don't worry, mate," he said. "I divvint think you'll survive the fall." He flipped Malcolm the rest of the way over. He screamed all the way down. Hit the Tyne hard.

John watched. Malcolm's body floated up to the surface, face down. The current carried it away. John left the bridge.

Chapter Twenty-Seven

Daniel went to see Steven, looking back over his shoulder all the way. He checked behind trees, parked cars, expecting *him* to emerge at any moment. To stand tall. The son of a bitch.

He hurried inside when Denise opened the door. "Daniel—what's the matter, pet?" she said, startled by his shifty movements. "You all right?"

"Where's Steven?"

"I'm through here, young'un," Steven called from the sitting room.

Daniel went through, straight to the windows, peered out through the blinds, checked the street.

"The matter with you, like?" Steven said.

Daniel left the window but couldn't take a seat.

"Thought you wanted to talk about Malcolm?"

"I do," Daniel said. "It's John. He's come back."

Steven snorted, shook his head. "Haddaway, man."

"His body was never found. He's not fuckin dead, and now he's back."

"Look, Daniel. Here, take a seat, will ye? You're

getting on me nerves, standing there all jumpy like that."

Daniel didn't want to, but he did. It was hard to settle. He could hear Denise busying herself in the kitchen. She was always in the kitchen, staying out the way.

"You're just upset, that's all. It's sad to think about, but Malcolm killed himself. We're all upset about it, we're all shocked by it, but that's just the way it is. Don't go looking for bogey men where there aren't any, all right?"

Daniel shook his head. "Malcolm didn't kill himself."

"Then maybe he got drunk and fell in."

"Fell in? Why would he be on the bridge in the first place?"

"Decided to visit someone in Gateshead? I divvint kna, man. All I do know is, I doubt this is what you're trying to make it."

"I'm not trying to *make* it anything. I want you to take it seriously."

"I am taking it seriously. It's very sad. It's a tragedy. But we all know Malcolm liked a drink—he got drunk and tripped into the Tyne, there's nowt to say he actually came off the bridge."

"Aye, the report says the impact killed him. He didn't drown."

"All right, all right, but still." Steven looked frustrated. "He tripped, like I said. Fell in. It's a real shame. Or else he got drunk and got lost in his thoughts and he threw himself in."

"Why would he even do that? That doesn't make any sense, Steven, and you know it."

"Whey, he'd never killed anyone before, had he? Could've been playing on his mind."

"He still hasn't. He was round the corner, he didn't have any part in what we did to John."

"He made the phone call. Lured him out."

"That's hardly enough to make him throw himself off a fucking bridge!" Daniel could hear Denise quieten in the kitchen, listening to their raised voices. "Why won't you admit it, man? Why won't you take it seriously?"

"You slit his throat, Daniel! People don't just get up and walk away from that!"

"He fucking did! Whether he's alive or not, he wasn't where we dropped him."

"You're just overthinking it. It was your first time an'all, wasn't it?"

"That's besides the point."

"Nah, son, I reckon that *is* the point."

Daniel closed his eyes, took a deep breath, ran his hands down his face. "Then where's Tina?"

Steven shrugged. "Maybe they broke up, before. She moved on. It happens."

"No one's heard from her."

"Why would they? Look, they broke up, Malcolm had too much to drink, dwelt on their ended relationship too long, and took a jump off the bridge. There ye gan, there's another theory for ye."

"I don't want theories, damn it. If that was the case, Tina would've come back. She'd be devastated. Why would they even break up, man? They weren't having any troubles. I can poke holes in all of your 'theories'."

"Daniel, son, thinking it's John come back from the dead is a bloody *theory*. Listen, when you've been in this game as long as I have, you divvint let yerself get worked up about anything until you need to. You're imagining a ghost, that's all. John's dead. He's not coming back for us. He can't. Wherever his body wound up, it's worm food by now. Here, if I'd known you were gonna get this jumpy, I wouldn't have let you do it yerself."

Daniel got to his feet, unable to believe what he was hearing.

"Where you goin now?"

"Home. I'm not staying here, listening to you spout that shite and not take this seriously. Our lives are at fuckin risk, man, and you couldn't give a toss."

"I'll give a toss if it ever comes time to give a toss," Steven said. "But it won't. Ye wanna put a bet on it?" He grinned.

Daniel sneered. "No. I fuckin don't. You can suit yerself, but I'm not takin any chances." He left the house, ignored Denise calling goodbye. Out on the street, he checked the road again. The path. The cars. The trees. He hurried back to his car, locked the doors once he was inside. Slammed his hand against the steering wheel. It was John. He knew it was.

Malcolm was dead, Steven didn't believe him, and he had no idea how to get in touch with Jock.

He was all alone.

Chapter Twenty-Eight

Jock was in the town of Hamilton, south of Glasgow. He lived alone on the end of a row of terraced houses. He didn't go out, and no one came to visit him. John parked over the road and watched the front door, the windows. Nothing to see. On the first day he'd wondered if he was even home. When it got dark, he could see the television's glow through the drawn curtains downstairs. John had chanced a couple of peeks through the windows, got an idea of the layout. He'd walked down the alley behind the house. There was a gate, a wall, a small shed in the yard. Nothing else to see.

He'd strike on the second night. No point waiting round. He drove away from the street, didn't want to stay in one place too long where he could be spotted. He busied himself in town, got something to eat. People stared at his scar. It had been the same in Newcastle. It would always be the same.

When it got dark he went back. Parked round the corner and went on foot the rest of the way. He checked the front. The television was glowing through the curtains again. He went round the back, tried the gate. Open. The back door led into the kitchen. John tried the handle. It wasn't locked. He was surprised, and instantly cautious. He'd been planning on kicking the door down, making a lot of noise to startle Jock, momentarily stun him, enough time for John to get the upper hand. Jock was a big lad, John didn't fancy his chances in a prolonged fight.

But the door was open. John got to thinking, his fingers still wrapped around the handle, had pushed it down only a couple of centimetres. Had Jock seen the car? Had he seen *him*? Was he waiting inside? This could be a trap. John braced himself. He pressed his shoulder to the door, opened it. Peered in. Gave his eyes a moment to adjust to the darkness.

The kitchen was clear. He listened. The television was on. The sound of gunshots. A car chase. John stepped through. Took his time. Cautious at every corner, every doorframe. He peered into the sitting room. The television played *The Professionals*. No one watched it.

Nothing else downstairs. Kitchen and sitting room. Jock wasn't in either. He was upstairs. He knew John was coming for him. If he didn't know it was John specifically, he knew someone had been watching him.

John held his breath, went up the stairs. Took his time, placed each foot lightly, wary of causing any creaks. He stuck to the wall. Kept his face turned up, watching the landing. The house was in darkness. The only light had been from the television.

There were three rooms. John guessed bedroom, spare room, bathroom. He went into the nearest first. The door was ajar. His heart was pounding. He wasn't happy about this. He was supposed to have the element of surprise. He was supposed to be the hunter. Now he felt like the prey.

All the while he looked, he listened, too. Half-expected footsteps to come up fast behind him. At this point, he wouldn't mind. He could spin, they could fight. It was the searching he hated, the anticipation.

The first room, the bedroom, was empty. He moved to the next. The spare. It held weights, a record player, nothing else. Only the bathroom remained.

John pushed the door open, stepped inside.

No one.

His eyes narrowed. Had he missed something? A room downstairs, perhaps? He didn't think so.

Jock wasn't home.

He stepped back out onto the landing, ran his finger along the scar at his throat, probed at its puckered edges. His eyes wandered upward. There was a door to the loft. Would Jock really go so far out his way to hide? Jock was a fighter. He wouldn't try to avoid anything. He would lie in wait, certainly, but he wouldn't hide out from the whole thing.

Still, there was nowhere else to look. John reached for the latch.

Downstairs, the back door opened and closed. He

heard movement in the kitchen, footsteps, something dumped onto the bench. A light was switched on. A key was put into the back door, it was locked. The footsteps moved through into the sitting room. *The Professionals* was ending. "Ah, shit," a voice said. It was Jock.

He'd been out. Shop, perhaps. John heard him move back through to the kitchen. John went down, stood in the doorway.

Jock's head turned slowly. "So you're still alive, are ye?"

"Looks that way," John said. "Else I'm a ghost come to say boo."

"Dinnae believe in them, pal. If they were real, this hoose would be fuckin full ay them."

The bag on the bench held beer bottles. Didn't look like he'd been out to get anything else.

"You always leave the back door open when you gan to the off license?" John said.

"People know better'n to come into my home."

John grunted. "I've already taken your worst, Jock. What have I got to be worried about?"

"That wisnae *my* worst. And you know that. We gonna get this over with, then?"

"I didn't come here to talk to you."

"I know exactly why you came here, pal." He took one of the beers from his bag, smashed the base against the counter. He held up the jagged edges, dripping beer. "Let's get it over with, ye Geordie bastard."

John didn't give him a chance to advance, to swing or jab with the broken bottle. He put his head down and charged, tackled Jock round the waist and slammed him back into kitchen sink. Jock slashed at his back with the glass. John slammed him again, right in the kidneys. Jock cried out. John came up, raised his head hard, busted Jock's face with the back of his skull. He knocked the broken bottle from his hand, then punched him in the gut and ribs.

Jock roared, spitting blood that ran into his mouth from his nose. He grabbed at John's face, tried to stick his thumbs into his eyes. He pushed off the bench, forced John back up against the wall.

John couldn't see. He clawed at Jock's wrists, at his thumbs. He kicked wild, hard. The thumbs fell away. John blinked stars from his eyes, kicked again. Jock coughed, reared back, punched John across the face. John slid down the wall, lost his balance. He could feel blood running down his back from the earlier cuts. Jock went back to the bottle. John forced himself up, rushed him from behind, slammed his head into the counter. John grabbed the bag full of beer bottles, swung them, hit Jock in the side of the face with them. He went down onto a knee. John swung the bag again, in a downward arc this time, brought it down right on top of Jock's head. Some of the bottles smashed. Blood poured from Jock's hairline.

Jock was down, dazed, but he was still trying to push himself up. He grabbed at John's legs, swung for them. John picked up the first broken bottle. He slashed at Jock's grasping fingers, then jabbed the glass into his neck. He left it embedded. Jock gasped, blood running down into his eyes, blood running from his neck. He pawed at the broken bottle. John threw him down onto his front. He stomped on the back of his neck. The glass crunched. John kept his foot in place, ground down on it. Jock's body squirmed. Blood poured from him, pooled beneath him, spread outward across the linoleum.

John kept his foot in place until the big bastard was dead. Unlike Jock and Daniel, he never left a body until he was sure it wasn't going to come back for him.

He stepped away, avoided slipping in the blood. He took one of the unbroken bottles of beer from the bag. Its glass body was wet, soaked in the contents of its smashed partners. John popped the top, took a drink. He spat it back out. After the fight, after being swung, it was flat.

Chapter Twenty-Nine

Daniel stayed in the house, kept the doors and windows locked, checked them regularly.

"What's the matter with you?" Mary said.

"Nowt, man, nowt," he said. Wouldn't tell her of his suspicions. She'd fucking love that. Love to know John was still alive and coming for her dear old husband.

He'd thought he'd seen something the night before. He'd been in his room, looking out onto the street below. A car parked opposite, under a tree. Perfect hiding spot. Daniel saw him though. The engine was off, the lights were off, but Daniel could see someone behind the steering wheel. A man's hands. Daniel stared, felt his heartbeat quicken, his mouth run dry. Five minutes passed. He'd convinced himself it was John.

Then a light came on in the doorway of the house opposite. The lass that lived there was stepping out, she walked down the pathway to the car, got into the passenger seat. She leaned over, kissed the driver.

The car started up, the headlights came on, the car drove away. Daniel breathed a sigh of relief, then resumed his vigilance.

It was daytime now, but he didn't feel any easier. Being stuck in the house was bad enough, but being trapped with Mary was torture. She could sense something was up. He wouldn't tell her anything, though. She wasn't an ally. She was an enemy. She went about her day, but he'd catch her shooting him looks out the corner of her eye whenever she passed by.

Daniel stayed upstairs for the most part, out of her way. Couldn't stand to look at her, and to feel her judging him for his behaviour.

But upstairs he got restless. Needed to keep checking the house, to make sure it was secure. He wouldn't be caught unaware. Steven might believe he was overreacting, but he was wrong. Steven wasn't reacting at all.

Daniel stared out the window and cursed himself for not finishing the job. He'd cut the bastard's throat, he hadn't expected him to get up from that. There'd been a lot of blood. He remembered the sinking feeling in his stomach the next day when Malcolm said he drove by and there was no sign of the body.

"What do you mean?"

"Nowt there," Malcolm said. "No police, no body, nowt."

He'd let them talk him down when they'd said if he'd managed to get up at all he'd likely just lain down and died somewhere else. He'd turn up eventually.

Daniel looked at his hands, remembered how they'd shaken on that night.

"Useless fuckin things…"

John should never have gotten up at all. Daniel should've gone deeper. He should've gone so deep he nearly took his fucking head off.

Instead, he'd gotten up, wandered off to somewhere safe, and secure, and healed, and now he was back. And Malcolm was dead. He'd be next.

He remembered cutting his throat. The feel of the blade slicing through the flesh, the handle getting slick. The sight of the blood. Daniel's skin had prickled. He'd wanted to retch, though he'd held it in, swallowed some of it back down. He was sure he'd gone deep enough. Hadn't cut through the windpipe, but at the very least he'd done enough damage for him to bleed out. Why hadn't he bled out?

Daniel had an epiphany then.

Dr Doug.

They'd asked him, he said he hadn't seen him. They'd believed him.

What if he'd lied?

Daniel left the house, didn't bother to tell Mary he was going out. He drove to Gosforth. The doctor was surprised to see him. "Daniel," he said. "Somethin wrong?"

"Can we have a word? Inside."

"Uh…" Doug looked back into the house. Daniel

could hear the television was on. Could hear the children laughing at something.

"It's important," Daniel said.

"I'm watching something with the family," Doug said.

"I'm not really asking, mate," Daniel said, firm. "It'll take five minutes."

"All right, howay then, in the kitchen."

Daniel followed him through. They sat at the table. They'd barely settled when Daniel asked, "Is John still alive?"

Doug's eyes widened momentarily before he was able to stop them, compose himself. Too late. He'd given himself away. Daniel already knew the answer. "Eh? John?"

"John Riddell."

"How would I know?"

"I wanna hear you say it, Doug."

"Say *what*?"

"Tell me what happened."

"I don't know what you're talking about, man, Daniel."

Daniel took a deep breath, pissed off. He slapped Doug across the table, grabbed him by the collar and slapped him again, dragged him over the top. He put his face close to Doug's. "Tell me what fucking happened."

"Please, man—me kids, they're right next door…"

"I divvint give a shit about your fuckin kids. Tell me what I wanna know." He raised his hand to slap him again, but Doug begged off.

"All right, all right," Doug said, bowing his head. "Aye, he's alive."

Daniel seethed. "What happened?"

"You didn't cut deep enough."

"*I fuckin know that*. How'd he get to you?"

"He walked here, holding his neck closed."

"He fucking *walked* here?" Daniel swallowed.

"Aye."

"And you put him back together."

"Yes."

"When we came here looking, was he here?"

Doug hesitated, then nodded.

"Where?"

"Upstairs, in the spare room. He was sleeping."

It would have been so easy. Just creep into the room, smother him with a pillow or something. Make sure this time the inhuman bastard's heart had stopped beating.

Daniel wanted to ask why Doug hadn't told them the truth. Why he'd helped John in the first place.

He didn't ask. It didn't matter.

He dragged Doug the rest of the way over the table so it toppled with a loud clatter. He tossed him onto the floor, punched him twice in the mouth, started kicking him. The sitting room door opened, Doug's family came into view. His wife started screaming. "What are you doing?"

The kids were both screaming, crying.

Daniel ignored them all. He kicked Doug harder.

"You stupid bastard! You stupid piece of fucking shit!" He grabbed him by the collar again, punched him over and over. The wife came forward, tried to get him off. Daniel back-handed her. She stumbled but didn't fall. Daniel got off her husband, grabbed her by a handful of hair from behind. "You silly bitch," he said. He threw her over the table. She rolled, hit the ground hard, slapping the side of her face off the linoleum.

Daniel stood over Doug, caught his breath. He looked at the kids in the doorway still. They were terrified of him. They turned, ran upstairs. He heard their bedroom door slam.

John was still alive. He'd fucking known it.

He left the house, hurried back to his car, sped over to Steven's house. He banged on the door. No answer. He peered in the window, but the blinds were drawn. He tried the handle. It wasn't locked. Daniel gritted his teeth. He pushed the door open. The smell hit him before he could call anyone's name. Daniel gagged. He covered his mouth and nose. The house stank of blood and waste. Daniel understood. It smelt of death.

His hands were shaking as he crept down the hall, silent as he could, listening to the house. The atmosphere within was thick, but it was still. He reached the sitting room, looked in. Steven was propped up in his chair. His throat was cut. Denise was on the sofa. Her throat was cut, too.

At the sight of them, Daniel panicked. He spun,

ran for the door. Tripped over his own feet, fell, managed to land on his hands. Pushed himself up and rushed out, stumbled out the door, down the pathway, back to his car.

He sped home. Mary gave a start as he burst into the house, slammed the door closed, locked it. She went to him. "For Christ's sake, Daniel—what's the matter with you?"

Daniel spun, eyes wide. He grabbed her by the face, forced her down to her knees, loomed over her. "Did you know? *Did you fucking know?*"

"Did I know what? Did I know *what*?" Mary grabbed at his wrists. "You're hurting me!"

Daniel let go of her, pushed her away. Mary stayed on the ground, propped up on an elbow, rubbing at her face. She looked at him, confused.

"Your boyfriend's still alive," he said.

Chapter Thirty

John hadn't killed Steven until he'd got the money he was owed, and then some. He'd figured he was due more than a little interest. It was in the boot of his car now, ready for when he left.

There were only two remaining.

He knew Daniel had found the bodies of Steven and Denise. He'd watched him, sitting in his car parked down the road. Grinned as he'd run from the house like there was a devil on his heels.

John had given him two days to sweat since then. He was watching the house. Daniel didn't leave, neither did Mary. No one came to see them. There was no one that could come to them; John had killed them. Daniel didn't have anyone else. Without Steven behind him, no one was interested in helping him out. And if they heard *why*, if they heard that Daniel had failed in killing John and now John had come back to return the favour, they wouldn't want anything to do with it. You try to kill a man and you *fail*? Well, you have to deal with the repercussions of that yourself.

The night was creeping in. John would make his move soon. He checked his throat in the mirror before it got too dark. Ran his finger along the scar.

Soon.

Chapter Thirty-One

Mary watched Daniel.

He was twitchy, nervous. Hadn't slept since he'd come back and told her that John had killed her parents.

He had a gun. Got it from his bedroom. She'd never known it was in the house. He clasped it tight. Never let go of it. He checked the windows, checked the doors, over and over. He hadn't eaten. Looked pale and skeletal.

Mary stayed out of his way. They hadn't spoken in the two days. He'd look at her out the corner of his eye sometimes, a hint of suspicion there. He'd unplugged the phone. Watched the street all night long.

He surprised her by talking. "There's a car out there hasn't moved," he said.

"There's probably a few," she said.

"I don't recognise this one."

"Okay. You keep a close eye on it, then."

He cocked his head. "Are you mocking me?"

"No, of course not." She tread lightly.

"Come look at it," he said, motioning for her to follow upstairs. "See if ye know it."

Mary obliged. They went through to his bedroom. She'd never been in it, not since he'd claimed it as solely his own. There wasn't much to see. The bed wasn't made. Dirty clothes were piled in a corner. She followed Daniel to the window. Daniel stiffened, went close to the glass, looked up and down the street. "Shit," he said.

"What? What is it?"

He shook his head. "It's gone." He chewed the inside of his cheek. "Okay, so, either it wasn't him, it was someone else and they've just moved on...or it *was* him and he's moving the car to not be suspicious. Maybe he saw me looking." Daniel scratched his head, stressed out.

Mary nodded along, not wanting to say anything against him.

"All right, all right." He bit his lip. "You can go back downstairs. If you hear something, give us a shout."

She nodded again, went to walk away. He reached out, grabbed her arm.

"I'm serious," he said. "You hear *anything*, you call for me."

Mary looked him in the eye. "He killed my parents, Daniel." She set her jaw. "Do you really think he's coming back to swoop in and carry me away?"

Daniel said nothing, but he didn't ease his grip, either.

Mary pulled her arm back, went downstairs.

She hadn't cried for her parents.

It wasn't that she wasn't sad. She was. She'd used up most of her tears on the miscarriage. She'd shed a few since her and John had been discovered, and a lot since she'd felt responsible for his 'death'. Anything else she'd had inside, it had dried up in the interim. Too much tragedy. She was numb. And now, with John coming to kill them both, she was preoccupied with other thoughts. Maybe she'd just let him. Her life was a mess. Was there anything worth saving?

She took a seat. She didn't watch the television, didn't read. All she could do was wait.

An hour later, Daniel came back downstairs. He checked the back door, checked the front.

"They're locked," Mary said. "They're always locked. Why wouldn't they be?"

"Aye, he killed your parents," Daniel said, continuing the conversation from upstairs as if there hadn't been a break, "but that doesn't mean I trust ye. You're a conniving bitch. I'll never make that mistake again. Maybe I should just shove you out onto the street, let him take you away. Reckon that would be the end of it? Give him you so he'll leave me alone."

"He doesn't want me."

"Oh, aye? And what makes you sure about that?"

"I set him up. I haven't heard a word from him all the while he was gone. He thinks I betrayed him. He *knows* I betrayed him. He's not coming here to play nice with me."

Daniel rolled his neck, cracked it. She saw the way his finger stroked the gun without his realising it, as if this act soothed him.

Something smashed in the kitchen. They both looked up, froze. Glass tinkled to the ground. Wind roared. It was a window. Daniel raised the gun. He looked at Mary. He was panting. His eyes bulged. He pointed the gun at the closed kitchen door.

Mary stayed where she was. Her fingernails dug into the arm of the sofa.

They waited. The door stayed closed. The wind howled against it. There was no movement in the kitchen.

Daniel motioned for Mary to stand. "Go open it," he said.

She shot him a look. "I'm not going to open it."

"I have the gun," he said. "I need both hands. Just open the fuckin door, man."

Mary got to her feet. She went to the door, took her time. Daniel was right behind her. He braced himself as she put her hand on the door handle. He spread his legs, extended the gun two-handed. Mary held her breath, pulled the door wide open so she was behind it, pressed to the wall, closed her eyes and braced herself for the sound of gunfire.

It didn't come.

She opened her eyes. Daniel had lowered the gun. He shook his head. Mary looked. The kitchen was empty. There was a rock on the floor, surrounded by shattered glass. It had been thrown through the window.

A distraction.

There was movement upstairs. Daniel's eyes shot to the ceiling. He raised the gun again. "*Shit*," he said. He went to the stairs. "He's in the house."

Mary followed. She didn't want to be left alone. John was close.

They went up. The movement they'd heard had ceased. There was no sound save for the howl of the wind again, getting louder now as they reached the landing. They could feel the cold of it. Another window, opened or smashed. They listened for anything else. Footsteps. Breathing. Heard nothing.

Daniel took three deep breaths then advanced, the gun held out before him. Mary could see the way his arm shook. Saw the hesitancy in his step. She heard a noise come from him, like a whimper. He was scared.

He opened the door of his bedroom, turned to go inside. An arm reached out, the hand wrapped around his wrist, took the gun from him. Daniel cried, startled. The hand struck him to the ground. John stepped into view. He was smiling. He looked down at the gun, tossed it to one side.

Fear had twisted Daniel's face. Mary had never seen such an expression before. John stepped closer to him.

"No!" Daniel was frantic, screaming. Waving his arms back and forth in front of himself like a small child about to have its arse smacked. "*No!*"

John hauled him to his feet, slapped him across the face with his open palm and then the back of his hand. He head-butted him. He punched him in the stomach. He raised his knee, slammed Daniel's face into it. Taking him by the collar, he threw him into the opposite wall. Daniel slid down it.

John turned, looked at Mary. Their eyes locked. He wasn't smiling now. She saw the scar across his throat. Her blood ran cold.

John turned back to Daniel. He kicked him, twice, then dragged him from the wall. He got down on top of him, pinned him with his body weight. He wrapped his hands around his throat, began to squeeze.

Mary watched. She saw Daniel's eyes rolling back in his head. Choked noises passed his lips. His tongue began to loll. John let go. Slapped him a couple of times, roused him. "Not yet," he said, then wrapped his fingers around his neck again.

Mary stepped past them. She picked up the gun John had discarded, turned. She raised it. Her hands and arms were shaking the same way Daniel's had.

John paid her no mind. He continued strangling her husband.

Mary squeezed the trigger. She flinched at the sound, almost deafened.

The bullet caught John high in the back. He released Daniel, fell forward. Daniel rolled onto his side, gagged, threw up a little. He rubbed at his neck.

John was still moving. He swallowed air, sounded like an animal as he did so. Sounded angry. He pushed himself up, to all fours. He looked back, saw Mary still holding the gun. Mary kept it raised. Kept it pointed at him. She tried to steady herself, to calm her breathing and her heartbeat.

John reached out for the wall, supported himself against it. He forced himself back up to his feet. He turned. Mary saw blood drip from the tips of the fingers on his left hand, running down his arm from the gunshot wound. He straightened. Took a step forward. There was murder in his eyes.

Mary squeezed the trigger. The bullet hit him in the chest. He stalled but didn't go down. Blood trickled from the corner of his mouth. He spat it out. Hatred burned in his eyes. He shook his head, as if unable to accept that she could stop him. He took another step forward. Mary fired the gun twice more. Both shots hit him in the chest.

He went down. Lay flat on his back, gasped for breath. His eyes stared straight up, flickered. Mary could see he was still trying to roll over, to push himself up. He grunted. He breathed his last.

Daniel was pressed against the wall. "You killed him," he said. He started to smile, to laugh. "Jesus Christ, man, you did it. You fucking did it! You killed him!"

Mary turned to Daniel. He turned to her. He was laughing harder now, the relief evident on his bloodied, bruised face. He held a hand out to her, calling her back to him, welcoming her home.

Mary raised the gun again. The laughter stopped.

All relief, all joy, left Daniel's face. Before he could say anything, she fired the gun. The bullet went through his hand, hit him in the shoulder. He cried out. She fired again. This time it went through his head. He slumped, slid down the wall. Blood streaked behind him.

Mary dropped the gun, kicked it away from herself. She stood in the centre of the carnage, smelled burning and blood. She closed her eyes, imagined that when she opened them again it would all be gone.

It wasn't.

But that didn't mean she had to stay.

The house was eerily silent now after all the noise, save for the sound of the wind still blowing through the broken glass.

She didn't have to stay. It was all over. Everyone was dead. Her parents, her husband. There was nothing keeping her here.

She thought about her brochures. Her dreams of escape. The moment had come.

She went to Daniel, searched his pockets for his car keys, then stopped.

Everyone she knew involved in this was dead, but not everyone that knew her. They'd know Daniel's car. She looked over at John's still form. They wouldn't know what he was driving. No one had.

She went to him, checked his pockets, avoided looking at his face while she did so. Couldn't help looking at the scar. She found the keys and her gaze wandered up. She gave a start. His eyes were still open. They were unseeing, but they were still as filled with hate and murder as they had been earlier.

Mary walked away from his dead stare. From her dead husband. She hurried downstairs and grabbed a coat, went out into the night. The keys belonged to a Citroën. She looked up and down the road. There were two. She went to the closest. The key didn't work. The other was further away. She went to it. It opened. She climbed inside, closed the door, put the key in the ignition. She wrapped her hands round the steering wheel and took a deep breath.

The car smelled like John. She remembered it vividly. It brought back many memories. He was on top of her. She was on top of him. They lay side by side.

The way he smiled at her that first time they spoke at her father's birthday party.

The way he'd looked at her tonight.

His dead eyes.

She exhaled, opened the window, and drove.

ACKNOWLEDGMENTS

This book wouldn't exist if I hadn't read some Richard Stark, and I wouldn't have read Richard Stark without Rob Pierce's recommendation, so I'm sending a big thank you Rob's way.

PAUL HEATLEY is the author of *Fatboy*, *Guillotine*, *The Motel Whore & Other Stories*, and the *Eye for an Eye* series, as well as over fifty short stories online and in print. He lives in the north east of England.

On the following pages are a few
more great titles from the
Down & Out Books publishing family.

For a complete list of books and to
sign up for our newsletter,
go to DownAndOutBooks.com.

Occam's Razor
Joe Clifford

Down & Out Books
June 2020
978-1-64396-106-4

Former NFL prospect Oz Reyes is summoned to Miami by his boss, Delma Dupree, who asks him to investigate what she calls "the wrongful imprisonment" of her stepson.

With the help of an ex-girlfriend her ex-convict brother, Oz uncovers a South Florida rarely seen, one crawling with shifty detectives, rogue assassins, and hard-drinking, sexual deviants—where no one and nothing is what it seems.

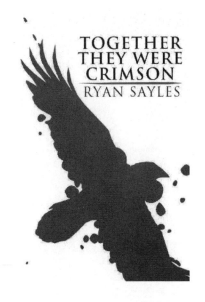

Together They Were Crimson
Ryan Sayles

Down & Out Books
July 2020
978-1-64396-037-1

An Angel of Mercy serial killer targets the elderly, but when a visitor catches her in the act, the Angel is forced to murder her.

Norm Braden, the victim's widower, is grieving for his lost wife and struggling to hold his family together.

Norm seeks revenge. The Angel seeks some form of completion she sees in him. And their cat-and-mouse game begins.

Helen Topaz, Henry Dollar
Part Three of the Trevor English Series
Pablo D'Stair

All Due Respect, an imprint of
Down & Out Books
May 2020
978-1-64396-100-2

Manufacturing threats of blackmail against himself, petty crook Trevor English convinces his lover, Helen, to pay off his fictional victimizer. But when Helen suggests that an investigator be brought in to find out who was behind the extortion, Trevor finds he must either maintain his intricate deception or end his affair—either option capable of spinning his life wildly out of his control.

Shotgun Honey Presents Volume 4: RECOIL
Ron Earl Phillips, editor

Shotgun Honey, an imprint of
Down & Out Books
May 2020
978-1-64396-138-5

RECOIL delivers stories that explore a darker side of remorse, revenge, circumstance, and humanity. Contributors: Rusty Barnes, Susan Benson, Sarah M. Chen, Kristy Claxton, Jen Conley, Brandon Daily, Barbara DeMarco-Barrett, Hector Duarte Jr., Danny Gardner, Tia Ja'nae, Carmen Jaramillo, Nick Kolakowski, JJ Landry, Bethany Maines, Tess Makovesky, Alexander Nachaj, David Nemeth, Cindy O'Quinn, Brandon Sears, Johnny Shaw, Kieran Shea, Gigi Vernon, Patrick Whitehurst.

Made in the USA
Columbia, SC
15 November 2020

24634257R00124